The Tenth Pupil

The Tenth Pupil

Constance Horne

RONSDALE PRESS

THE TENTH PUPIL
Copyright © 2001 Constance Horne

RONSDALE PRESS
3350 West 21st Avenue
Vancouver, B.C., Canada
V6S 1G7

Set in Minion: 12 pt on 16
Typesetting: Julie Cochrane
Printing: Hignell Printing, Winnipeg, Manitoba
Cover Art: Ljuba Levstek
Cover Design: Julie Cochrane

Ronsdale Press wishes to thank the Canada Council for the Arts, the Government of Canada through the Book Publishing Industry Development Program (BPIDP), and the Province of British Columbia through the British Columbia Arts Council for their support of its publishing program.

CANADIAN CATALOGUING IN PUBLICATION DATA
Horne, Constance.
    The tenth pupil

    ISBN 0-921870-86-8

    1. Logging — British Columbia — Vancouver Island — History — Juvenile fiction. 2. Vancouver Island (B.C.) — History — Juvenile fiction. I. Title.
PS8565.O6693T46 2001   jC813'.54   C2001-910228-3
PZ7.H7824Te 2001

ACKNOWLEDGEMENTS

The author thanks Gordon Horne for his research, map-making and computer skills.

The Tenth Pupil is a work of fiction. Mellor's Camp and its georgraphy are imaginary, but typical of the numerous small logging outfits operating in British Columbia in the early 20th century.

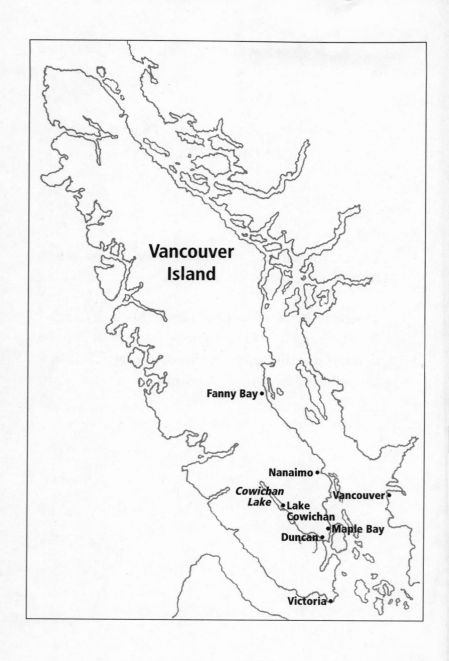

Vancouver Island

Fanny Bay •

Nanaimo •

Cowichan Lake • Lake Cowichan

Vancouver •

Duncan •

• Maple Bay

Victoria •

1

Mellor's Camp

Not a drop of rain had fallen in the Cowichan Valley on Vancouver Island in the first three weeks of August, 1934. While the deep woods held some moisture, logged-off hillsides, like the one Trudy Paige sat on, were bone dry. With two other girls, she was on spark watch. Their job was to protect the dry grass from catching fire from the sparks sent out by the Shay engine as it pulled logs from the woods to the dump below them. They had been on duty since lunch time and now, at 4:30, were waiting for the last train of the day.

Mary was lying on her back with her straw hat over her eyes.

"I hate this job," she said. She shook an ant off her right

arm. "I'm hot and I'm bored and the grass pricks my legs and the ants bite me and I'm probably going to die from sunstroke and besides I'm thirsty."

Trudy reached around the stump she was leaning on and lifted a sealed jar of lemonade out of the pail of water.

"There's just a mouthful left," she said.

Mary uncovered one eye. "I don't want that!" she said. "It's cooked by now!"

"Can I have it?" asked Frieda. Copying Trudy, she had turned down the brim of her white gob hat to protect her eyes from the brilliant sun. Now she flipped it back and stared eagerly at the bottle.

Trudy hesitated a moment and then passed the jar to the younger girl.

"Might as well finish it," she said. As she turned around again, she gasped. "Look! The kids are going swimming! The lucky stiffs!"

Mary sat up with a jerk. Her long braid was full of dried grass stalks almost the same colour as her hair. She brushed at them angrily where they scratched her neck. Trudy was glad her Mum had cut her hair short at the beginning of the hot spell.

"Where's that dumb train?" Mary asked. She glared at the railway bridge that linked the camp to the woods where the loggers worked. "It will soon be supper time and we won't get a chance to swim."

The three girls watched enviously as a group of barefooted children ran along the plank road on the other side of the Copper River. In a minute they were hidden by the bunk house. They could hear the shouts as their brothers and sisters splashed into the swimming hole just where a stream flowed into the river. Even with the water at its lowest, the pool would be deep enough to cool them off.

Mary flopped down again with a groan. Trudy continued to stare over the camp. Heat waves rose from the corrugated tin roof of the sawmill and made her feel hotter than ever. She imagined herself slipping into the pool. The water would be cool because the stream was still shaded for its whole length by trees that the loggers had left on its banks. Trudy was glad that the camp owner loved to fish as much as she did. That's why he had left trees to protect both this stream and Black Creek on the southern side of the camp. In contrast, both sides of the river had been logged right to the edge of the bank to make room for the camp buildings.

Trudy's Dad was the one who got permission from Mr. Mellor to build a small breakwater to make a pool at the bend of the river where the stream entered. Dad knew how much his kids missed living on Cowichan Lake in Drew's Floating Camp #5. There they could swim and fish and boat whenever they wished. Here they had a raft, but Trudy missed the rowboat. It was still on the lake and sometimes the family went back to the old site and rowed to a favourite fishing place. That camp was gone, though. Three years ago, when all the timber that could be reached by rail had been logged, Mr. Drew sold out to Frank Mellor. Drew moved to his other property on the opposite shore of Cowichan Lake. All the buildings had been towed across to the north side. It was now called Drew's Camp #6. Most of the loggers and their families had gone to the new site. Tom Paige, Trudy's father, decided to stay on the south side and work for the new owner. Frank Mellor planned to use trucks to log the steep hillsides that the railway couldn't reach. He built his camp on land close to the mountains. So now the Paiges lived in this small, isolated camp five miles inland from their old home and a very long way from Milton, a mill town at the east end of Cowichan Lake.

The train whistle sounded.

"At last!" said Mary.

The girls scrambled up. Each dipped a piece of sacking into the water pail. They moved apart into a line paralleling the new gravel road and the railway track. Trudy was on the far left, opposite the sawmill and nearest to the railway bridge. Frieda was in the middle across from the bunk house and Mary on the right closest to the railway shed where the train would finally stop for today. As she watched the Shay engine creep across the old bridge, Trudy saw sparks being deflected downwards from the spark catcher on top of the smokestack. Most fell harmlessly on to the track, but just one escaping and starting a fire could mean disaster. No doubt the Japanese family would also be on the watch. They lived on the other stream between the old railway bridge and the half-finished truck bridge. In the camp there were plenty of fire-watchers: the men at the mill, the cook and his flunkeys at the bunkhouse, the blacksmith and the mothers and children in the six houses across the river.

There were two flatcars attached to the engine. When it stopped with a screech at the main log dump just this side of the bridge, the first car tilted and logs rolled with a clatter to the base of the A-frame. The second car dumped its load at the sawmill. For a few minutes, the noise of falling logs drowned out the scream of the saw. While he waited, the engineer waved to the girls on the hill. Then the fireman threw in the last log to get up enough steam for the short run to the railway shop. Sparks flew from the stack.

Trudy ran down a few steps to swat one ember with her wet cloth and then up again to deal with another. She looked around for more. Frieda was standing over a tiny plume of smoke that Trudy could see plainly even from several yards away.

"What are you doing?" she shrieked. She ran toward Frieda. "Put it out!"

The girl seemed to wake from a dream. She beat the miniature flame. Trudy gave it a final stomp with both running shoes as Mary ran over.

"Are you crazy?" asked Mary, looming over the shorter girl.

Frieda looked up at Trudy for protection. Her cheeks

reddened. "I just wondered if it really would start a fire," she said. "I wasn't going to let it burn."

"You're nuts!" said Trudy.

The sun had just slipped down behind the mountains in the west and the hillside no longer dazzled the eyes. The girls patrolled the whole area. There was no fire. They ran down the hill, over the new road, past the Shay engine panting on the tracks and on to the old road that led to a bridge over the Coppermine River. Just before the bridge, as they were passing the small schoolhouse, Trudy's dog ambled out from under the porch.

"Good boy, Shaggy," said Trudy, bending to stroke his black fur.

Frieda placed the water pail against a bridge post where tomorrow's gang could find it, then caught up to the others. They had slowed down to walk at the old dog's pace.

"You're all mixed up, you dumb dog," said Mary. "School doesn't start till next week."

"I wonder who our new teacher will be," said Frieda. "Does your Mum know yet, Trudy?"

"Not for sure," answered Trudy. "Mum wants a girl from one of the farms down the road past Milton."

"A girl! Oh, goody!" said Frieda.

"Well, she might be allowed," Trudy answered cautiously. "Only there's lots of men school teachers who want the job and she's just new. This would be her first school."

They stopped on the bridge, which was now in shadow.

Hanging over the rail, they stared at the water flowing sluggishly toward the lake. In front of them on the far bank, just steps from the bridge, was a small house used as a teacherage. Like the other houses, it was painted grey with red trim and had a shingle roof and a porch. But it was just half the size of the family homes which each had one big room, a scullery and two small bedrooms. The teacherage had stood empty since Mr. Wells left in June. Trudy thought it looked forlorn.

"Never mind, little house, somebody will soon move in," she said happily. She twirled around on her toes. "I can't wait for school to start!"

"It will seem funny without Helen and Anne," said Mary. "I wish Mrs. Mellor hadn't taken them to Vancouver."

"She had to," argued Trudy. "Helen's going to high school and Anne couldn't stay here with just her Dad. Anyway, Eddie Dodd will be starting grade one, so that makes ten kids."

"Nine," said Frieda.

"Ten! Count them." Trudy pointed at Mary, at herself and at Frieda. "Three Johnsons, three Paiges, three Carleys, and Eddie. That's ten."

"My brother's quitting school," Frieda announced. "He's starting as whistle punk tomorrow."

Trudy snatched off her hat and pushed her fingers through her bangs until the hair stood straight up. "He can't quit!" she said. "You need ten kids to get a teacher! We won't be able to have school. Tell your Mum he has to come."

Frieda grimaced. "It won't do any good. Len hates school. He's just been waiting to get into the woods. Besides, Dad wants him working."

She walked away and the other two quickly jumped to either side of her, forcing her onto the dry grass in the middle of the road while they marched along the planks.

"Everybody's going to be mad at you Carleys!" warned Mary.

"What are we going to do?" asked Trudy. "We have to have a school."

"Maybe nine will be enough," said Frieda.

"Not unless our parents pay for the teacher," answered Trudy. "The Department of Education only pays if there's ten kids or more."

Mary groaned. They all knew their parents had no extra money.

Trudy stopped opposite Mrs. Sutton's house, the first in the row. She put her hands on her hips and frowned at the ground in concentration.

"We'll just have to find another kid," she said.

The other two turned and stared at her.

"Where?"

They all looked along the street of identical houses. The Sutton children were all grown up. Then came the Carleys, the Paiges, the Dodds, the Lawsons, who just had a tiny baby, and the Johnsons. Farther along, at the bend in the river, was the two-storey owner's home.

"What other kid?" repeated Mary.

"I don't know," wailed Trudy, "but I want to go to school!"

2

Shaggy Fields

Mrs. Paige was as upset as Trudy when she heard the news. She was coating the fish fillets with flour for supper. She held her dusty hands over the plate while she stared blankly at her daughter.

"I just had a letter from the Department of Education in Victoria," she said. "They've appointed Miss Shirley Lewis to our school."

"Good!" interrupted Trudy.

"Yes, but I've got to fill in lots of forms." She gestured with her chin to the brown envelope on the sideboard. "I have to send a list of the children on the register."

Before Trudy could answer, Karl burst into the room with Muriel at his heels. Both were still dripping wet.

Muriel grabbed him by the arm when he skidded into the table.

"Mum, Karl wouldn't come out when the quitting whistle blew," she said over his head.

"I never heard it," Karl replied. He squirmed away.

"Yes, you did! You're not deaf!"

"Quiet, you two," said Mum. "Go and get dressed. And Trudy, you peel the potatoes. Your Dad will soon be here for his supper."

"What's wrong?" asked Muriel. "Why are you mad?"

"We'll talk about it when your Dad gets here. Go and get dressed."

Muriel and Karl both looked to their older sister for an answer. Trudy just shrugged and picked up the paring knife.

Karl, who would be going into grade two, didn't care that school might not open. But the rest of the Paiges were really worried. Both of the parents had grown up in logging camps. Their education had varied from one-room schools to correspondence lessons to no school at all. Both were anxious for their own children to get a better education. Before Tom Paige had agreed to work for the new outfit, Mr. Mellor assured him there would be a school for Trudy and Muriel.

"My own daughters will be going," he said. "It'll be small for a couple of years till we get going, but once we're logging these hills with trucks the place will grow like blazes.

We'll have a town here and a high school one of these days. Just wait and see."

"It's Mr. Mellor's fault for sending his girls to town," said Mum. "He should bring in another family."

"He won't be hiring for months. Not till the bridge is finished and he's got a couple of trucks," answered her husband. "Why don't you just register Len Carley? No one will know. We haven't seen any inspector from Victoria in two years."

"It's too risky," said his wife.

"Why?" asked her husband. "If the inspector does come you can say Len just quit."

"He'd still close down the school."

"I suppose so."

There was a long, glum pause. Trudy thought hard. How could they get ten kids? "Hey!" she shouted suddenly, "Maybe Mrs. Dodd will send Bertie."

Her mother was doubtful. "He's only just turned five," she said. "But I'll try. Something has to be done. I'll go and see her this minute."

Mrs. Dodd said no. Maybe in the spring. Right now Bertie was too young.

By the next day, everyone in camp was discussing the problem of the school. Counting the six families, Mr. Mellor and his sons and the men on the two crews, there were nearly seventy-five opinions on the subject. That evening all the mothers and most of the kids gathered on the Paiges' front porch. They talked for some time without finding a solution. Trudy was sitting on the bottom step with Shaggy at her feet. She looked up at the women. Mrs. Johnson was biting her lip. Mrs. Carley looked embarrassed. Mrs. Dodd's mouth was set in a stubborn line. Mrs. Sutton and Mrs. Lawson both looked as though they would help if they could. Her own mother looked glum. Tears filled Trudy's eyes. She bent over Shaggy to hide them. She picked up his floppy ears and turned his face toward her.

"I guess you won't be coming to school this year," she said sorrowfully.

Suddenly, she jerked upright. The dog yelped at the pull on his ears.

"Shaggy!" she exclaimed.

"Shaggy what?" asked her mother.

"Shaggy goes to school every day. Put him on the register."

Every eye was on Trudy. For a moment nobody spoke.

"A dog?" asked Mrs. Johnson.

"Wow! Good thinking, Trudy!" said Mary.

Then everyone talked at once.

"We can't do that!"

"It's only for a year."

"No one will ever know."

"The teacher will."

"She probably wants this job pretty bad. She'll go along."

"Enrol a dog!"

Soon all the children and women were giggling and laughing.

"Shaggy Paige," said Trudy. "What grade will he be in?"

"Grade three," answered Muriel, "because he's nine years old, like me."

Their mother shook her head. "Not Paige," she said. "We won't register him next year. Someone in Victoria might notice he's missing."

"You could say he died," suggested Mary.

That sobered the women. None of them thought that the death of a child, even an imaginary one, was funny. Mrs. Sutton broke the sudden silence.

"Use my family name," she said. "Call him Shaggy Fields."

"We can't!" repeated Mrs. Carley.

"We can and we will!" declared Mrs. Paige. "I'll send in the forms tomorrow. We'll open the school next Tuesday."

That night it rained heavily. By morning, it had turned to a light drizzle. No one complained. The kids were happy because it meant no spark duty. The loggers were happy because the woods operation would not shut down and put them out of work.

Mrs. Paige organized a clean-up of the schoolhouse and teacherage and all the women and children helped. When both buildings were clean, the women stocked the teacherage kitchen with pots, pans and dishes. The last teacher had eaten his meals in the cookhouse with the loggers. Miss Lewis wanted to do her own cooking.

The last thing Trudy did that day was to print a message on the blackboard: WELCOME MISS LEWIS TO MELLOR'S CAMP SCHOOL.

When everyone else had gone home, Trudy and her mother stood on the school porch and took a last look around. Across the river, the polished windows of the teacherage shone in the evening light. In front of them, not a single weed or scrap of paper marred the surface of the narrow strip of earth between the porch and the road.

Mum clasped her hands together under her chin. "I hope she likes it here," she said.

"Who? Miss Lewis?" asked Trudy. "Why wouldn't she?"

"Well, there is that little matter of Shaggy Fields," answered her mother dryly.

"Oh, that!" said Trudy.

Her mother laughed. "Yes, that! Come on. We won't worry about it till we have to." On the bridge, she said, "How about a picnic tomorrow? The last of the summer."

"Good! Can we go to the falls and fish?"

"Why not?"

Next morning, Dad and Mum got up early to do the Sunday chores before they set out on the picnic. By ten o'clock the whole Paige family was tramping along the path by the stream. Dad led the way carrying two rods and the tackle box. In the knapsack on his back a tin kettle and a small grate rattled together. Trudy carried her own rod and had a cloth bag full of enamel cups and plates slung over her shoulder. The food was stowed in Mum's knapsack and

Muriel carried the creel for bringing back the fish. At first, Karl ran ahead to see what was around the bend or lagged behind to look at something or walked beside one of his sisters. Finally, he settled down to plod steadily in his father's footsteps.

After they had walked about ten minutes, no noise reached them from the camp. Trudy loved the Sunday quiet of the woods. Trains, donkey engines, axes and whistles all were idle. The only sounds were the murmur of the stream, the occasional call of a bird or a rustle in the underbrush as a small animal passed. The smells were different, too. In camp, there was a new-wood smell to everything. Out here in the forest, things smelled old and natural. Even the odour of decay was not unpleasant because you could see new life growing out of the rotting stumps. Suddenly Muriel jumped when a small branch fell on the path in front of her.

"What did that?" she asked fearfully. "A bear?"

"Don't worry," answered her Dad. "Any bear that comes across this noisy parade is going to hightail it in the other direction pretty fast."

In another five minutes they came to the first pool where they often fished. Karl ran ahead and jumped down from the path to a flat rock. He stopped abruptly. A Japanese man had a line in the water. He kept his back to them as he slowly trolled the hook. Beside him, in an eddy, was a string of fish he'd already caught.

Dad pulled Karl back up to the path and Mum herded him and the girls farther along.

"I see they're biting, Ken," Dad called to the man.

He turned and nodded without speaking.

"We're going higher up," Dad said. "Good fishing!"

The man didn't answer.

"What's eating him?" murmured Dad.

When they were out of earshot, Trudy said, "Did you see? He had four rainbows — real beauties!"

"Yes," said Mum. "The Japanese are good fishermen."

Dad laughed. "Too good! That's why they're loggers now!"

"What do you mean?" asked Trudy.

"All the Japanese we have here used to be commercial fishermen up the coast. But they caught so many fish, there wasn't much left for the others, so the white fishermen asked the government to cut the Japanese out."

"I hope this guy left some fish for us!" said Karl fiercely.

"Why doesn't he fish in Black Creek?" asked Muriel. "That's where he lives."

They could now hear the falls. There were two long drops, one about twice as high as the other. Each had a pool at the bottom where fish found plenty to eat. The lower one had a wide rock ledge where Mum could set out the picnic lunch and keep an eye on Karl and Muriel. They always clamoured to use the rods first, but soon got bored and left the serious fishing to Mum, Dad and Trudy.

As usual, Mum caught the first fish, but Trudy caught the biggest. She was downstream from Dad and had cast into a pool under the opposite bank. It looked like the perfect place for fish, but none of the family had ever caught one there. Most casts either went too far and hit the bank or fell short into the current of the stream. Trudy took off her running shoes, rolled her slacks up to her knees and stood on a flat rock with the water lapping her toes. She cast twice to test her aim. The third try went right into the pool and immediately she felt a strike on her line. Quickly, she reeled in. No fish. But now she knew there was one in there. She waded out into the stream, aimed carefully and dropped the lure in exactly the same spot.

"Nice cast," said Dad quietly from somewhere to her left.

Before she could turn to grin at him, her line ran out. She'd hooked a fish! She leaned back and the tug on the line almost pulled her off balance. She heard Dad sloshing toward her in his waders.

"Wow! It's a big one," he said. "Give it some slack."

The fish tore off downstream until Trudy checked it. Then it fought its way upstream. When Trudy jerked the line, it leapt into the air. Trudy staggered. She splashed as much as the fish as it re-entered the water.

"It's a steelhead!" said Dad.

From behind her, Trudy heard Mum urging her to hang on.

"It's a monster," yelled Karl.

"Don't lose it! Don't lose it!" begged Muriel.

"Hand me the net, Karl," said Dad.

The fish fought valiantly and Trudy played it expertly in spite of aching arms. Finally she reeled it in. When it made its last leap, Dad slipped the net under it.

He and Trudy and Karl stood gazing at the silver form flapping in the net.

"What a beauty, girl," said Dad.

"What a whopper!" said Karl.

Trudy grinned at them both. Then she realized that her feet and legs were freezing cold. She waded back to shore and stomped her feet to warm them. Dad removed the hook and held the fish against her. It stretched from her waist to her ankle.

"We forgot the camera," moaned Muriel.

"Never mind," said Mum. "We won't forget this fish in a hurry!" Inspired by that success, Trudy could have spent many more hours on the stream. She hardly wanted to take time to eat the trout Mum had caught. But the woods became dark early in the shadow of the mountain. Many animals, especially cougars, began to hunt in the dusk. Mum liked the family to be safe at home before that.

Trudy insisted on carrying the creel with her fish in it. All the way home, she relived in her mind her battle with the steelhead. It was the biggest fish she'd ever caught. She wished her grandfather lived closer so she could tell him the story. It wasn't until she was again walking along the road toward their own house that she even thought about school and the problem of Shaggy Fields. Ahead, on their front porch, sat a strange young woman. She wore a navy blue suit and a white blouse. Her long brown hair was neatly braided. As they approached, she stood up and smiled nervously.

"Mrs. Paige?" she asked. "I'm Miss Lewis, your new teacher."

3

Saved!

The teacher stayed for supper. Miss Lewis had been fishing since she was Trudy's age, so there were lots of fish stories told as they ate the day's catch. They hardly mentioned school. Trudy kept waiting for her mother to tell about Shaggy Fields. She knew she wouldn't be able to sleep that night unless she knew whether Miss Lewis would be staying.

Mrs. Paige walked the teacher back to her house to make sure she had everything she needed. She was gone a long time. Trudy ran to meet her when she returned.

"What did she say about Shaggy?" she asked.

"She wasn't pleased," answered her mother.

"But will she stay?"

"She agreed to meet with the other mothers tomorrow. Then she'll decide."

The next morning, Mary and Frieda waited on the bridge with Trudy while the mothers and Miss Lewis met in the school. The girls leaned on the rail and watched the water flowing toward them and curling against the pilings. Mary thought the teacher would agree to stay, Frieda thought she wouldn't. Trudy focussed on two willow twigs floating down the river. If the bigger one reached the bridge first, the teacher would stay. If it was the little one, she'd go. Both twigs drifted on to the right bank and stuck there. Before they floated free, the mothers came out.

The girls studied their faces. They weren't laughing and chatting, but they didn't look sad.

"She's staying, isn't she?" asked Trudy.

Her mother nodded. Mrs. Dodd had faithfully promised to send Bertie to school in January. Shaggy Fields could then be dropped from the register and the deception would never be discovered. Everyone was sure that an inspector would not visit Mellor's Camp before then.

Shaggy came to school every day. If the weather was fine, he settled in a corner of the porch. If it rained, he went underneath. Sometimes he played with the kids at recess, sometimes he just lay and watched the games. By the end of the month, everyone had forgotten that he was anything but a dog.

Stan Rowe was the first one in camp to hear the bad

news. He was a friend of the Paige family, so he knew how unhappy they would be if the school closed. Besides being a logger, Stan was the first-aid man for the camp. On the first Tuesday in October at about ten o'clock in the morning, he was in the little infirmary next to the office at one end of the bunkhouse. With him was one of the Japanese, Kenta Nakano. He had cut his arm a week before. Stan was renewing the dressing for him when the phone rang in the office. Stan answered it. He listened, turned pale and swore.

"Thanks, I'll tell her," he said and hung up.

"Bad news?" asked Mr. Nakano.

Stan groaned as he strapped tape over the new bandage.

"That was the teacher at Camp Six. There's a guy from Victoria on his way here to inspect the school."

"He's coming today?" asked Mr. Nakano.

"Yeah! Talk about bad timing! We thought he'd come in the spring, if he came at all. There. Your cut is healing nicely. Come and see me in a week." He put away his supplies. "I've got to go and warn the teacher. And hide that darn dog!"

They walked down the steps together. Mr. Nakano hurried off in one direction and Stan in the other. When Stan knocked on the school door, Trudy opened it. Miss Lewis was doing arithmetic at the board with Al Johnson and Nick Carley. She stepped out on the porch, leaving the door open. The children all overheard the message Stan brought. Inspector Fallis would arrive that afternoon! Trudy's hand shook so much that she dropped her pencil. She and Mary gazed at one another in horror.

Miss Lewis looked in.

"Go on with your work," she said in a shaky voice. "Trudy, you keep order. I'm going to find your mother."

No one did any work and Trudy did not even try to keep order. She had as much to say as anyone as they speculated about what would happen.

"I hope he does close the school," said Nick. "I'll go fishing every day."

"No you won't, you dope," answered Mary. "You'll have to do lessons at home."

"Or maybe," said Trudy, "they'll send us to Camp Six every day. How'd you like to spend over an hour travelling each way? You'd never get time to fish!"

"Maybe we'll be sent away to live somewhere else, like the Mellor girls," said Frieda, fearfully.

"I wouldn't go," declared Al.

"Oh, yes, you would!"

They were still arguing when Miss Lewis came back. She dismissed them for lunch although it was only eleven o'clock.

Two hours later, the teacher and the school trustee had worked out a strategy. Miss Lewis was going to tell the inspector that Shaggy Fields was away sick. If necessary, Mrs. Paige would say that he'd been sent to the hospital in Duncan. The children were all to keep quiet unless the inspector asked them a direct question.

Nick sat by the window and kept a lookout. After a couple of false alarms, he spotted the inspector's car just before two o'clock. Trudy got up to open the door.

"Wait till he knocks," whispered Miss Lewis.

Trudy nodded. She remembered that this visit was supposed to be a surprise.

A knock! Trudy took a deep breath and opened the door. The man standing there was short and round and had a smile on his face. He wasn't at all the monster she'd been expecting.

"Good afternoon," he said. "May I come in?"

Blushing, Trudy stepped aside and allowed him to pass her. Leaving the door open, she collapsed into her seat. She folded her trembling hands together and rested them on the desk. Was this going to be the last day of school?

The visitor greeted Miss Lewis and introduced himself.

"I'm Mr. Fallis from the Department of Education. Most years I get so tied up with business or held up by bad weather that I never get to these out-of-the-way schools. So, this year I decided to start with them."

Miss Lewis introduced him to the class. They stood up and greeted him politely, as they'd practised.

"Sit down! Sit down!" he said, with a smile. "Go on with your work. I'll come round and check it in a few minutes, after I talk to your teacher."

Everyone pretended to be working, but they were all listening to what was being said at the front of the room.

The inspector sat down at the teacher's desk.

"Let me see the register, please," he said.

Trudy gasped and ducked down to hide her frightened face behind Frieda. All the children sat still, barely breathing, while the man examined the roll.

"Ten children, I see," he said. He turned and smiled at Miss Lewis who was standing slightly behind him with her hands clasped tightly together. "You're lucky — just enough to have a school. Children, attention, please!" They all jumped. "Put down your pencils. Sit up straight. Hands behind your backs. Good! Now, answer the roll, so I can match names with faces."

He went through the names from Eddie Dodd in grade one to Trudy Paige in grade six. Twice he had to ask a child to speak up. Soon he would ask why everyone was so nervous. Trudy glanced at the teacher. Frightened eyes stared from her pale face. She had crossed her arms and was holding her elbows so tightly that her knuckles were white dots on her blue dress.

"And Shaggy Fields," said Mr. Fallis. "Where is Shaggy?" No answer.

He looked at Miss Lewis. "Where is Shaggy?" he asked. She opened her mouth but no sound came.

She can't tell a lie, thought Trudy in despair. Then to her horror, she heard a step on the porch. For a moment she thought her dog was going to answer to his name.

Instead it was a boy who appeared in the doorway. He was dressed as if for a party in long pants, a white shirt and tie and polished shoes. He carried school books bound together with a leather strap.

"I am Shigi," he said.

"Shee gee" sounded very much like Shaggy. All the children turned to stare at him. It was the Japanese boy from the family who lived on Black Creek. They had sometimes seen him at the store or riding in a truck through camp, but none of them knew his name or how old he was.

"You're late," said the inspector sternly.

The boy bowed.

"Well, come in, come in. Take your place, Shaggy Fields. You have already embarrassed your teacher and your classmates."

Trudy secretly pointed to the empty desk next to hers. The boy walked in and stood beside it.

"Sir, my name is Shigi Nakano," he said politely, but firmly.

Mr. Fallis frowned at Miss Lewis.

"Tut! Tut! Is Shaggy Fields your attempt at Anglicizing his name? I strongly disapprove of that practice. People come to Canada from all over the world. We should honour their differences, not try to change them."

"Yes, Mr. Fallis," answered Miss Lewis in a whisper.

The inspector turned back to the boy who was still standing.

"Spell your name for me."

"S H I G I   N A K A N O."

The man printed it on the roll and then looked up. "You were born in Canada, I suppose?"

"Yes sir, at Storm Inlet up near Prince Rupert."

"That's all right then. Japanese nationals can't attend school but children born in Canada can. Sit down. Open your notebook. I'm going to look at everyone's work now."

He started with grade one, which gave Trudy's beating heart time to calm down. She exchanged wide grins with Mary. Ten kids! They had a legal school!

4

The Tenth Pupil

Shigi Nakano had a great hunger, a hunger for knowledge. He wanted to know everything. In the school for Japanese children at Storm Inlet, he had always made top marks. His mother, Yuko, was very proud of him. She dreamed that one day he would go to university. Shigi shared her dream.

Storm Inlet was a fishing port and cannery town. The village consisted of three distinct areas: one for the white people, one for the Japanese and one for the native people. Each had its own stores, school and community activities. There was little interaction among the groups, even though most of the men were fishermen and the women like Shigi's mother worked in the cannery. Shigi remembered that for him and Yumi, his little sister, the Japanese section of Storm Inlet had been a good place to live. Although the work was seasonal, their parents made enough money to live comfortably. There were lots of children to play with. At least once a year, the Nakanos went to Vancouver to visit friends in Little Tokyo on Powell Street.

In 1930 everything had changed for the worse.

The Canadian Government cancelled the fishing licenses of many of the Japanese on the British Columbia coast. That year, Kenta Nakano tied up his boat and worked for a white fisherman. The next season no one would hire him. Along with many other Japanese, he decided he must give up fishing. Leaving his family in Storm Inlet, he did odd jobs in logging camps for a year. When he found a permanent job at Mellor's Camp, he moved his family south to join him.

There were only four other Japanese in the camp. All were bachelors, so there were no friends for Shigi and Yumi. The Japanese built two houses, one for the men and one for the Nakano family, on the south bank of Black Creek. Because they knew from bitter experience that they were tolerated, not liked, by white people, they kept to themselves as much as possible.

For Shigi, the greatest loss was that he couldn't go to school. When his family arrived in January, Ken Nakano had asked his boss on the maintenance gang when school would open.

"For a Jap kid? Never!" said Bill Carley. "Your kind don't go to school with white kids."

Shigi and his mother were hurt and angry. They wanted to fight. Kenta consulted the other Japanese men. They shrugged their shoulders.

"*Shigataganai*?" they said. "What can you do? If you make a fuss, you'll get us all fired. The way to get on with white people is to keep out of their way. Be patient. Some day the boy will get his chance."

Shigi wanted to go to school now, not some time in the distant future! But his parents agreed with the men. They had already lost their boat, their house and their livelihood. They must be patient. Yuko suggested sending Shigi to Japan to live with her parents and be educated there. Kenta was against it. He had grown up in the household of his own stern grandfather. Coming to Canada had been an escape from a country of class distinctions and strict rules.

"Our son is better off in this country," he said. "Some day we Japanese will be accepted as citizens. In the meantime, wife, you must help the boy with his lessons."

"I cannot teach him English," protested Yuko.

"We will have English books sent from Vancouver," he answered. "You teach him in Japanese. It is the best we can do for now."

Months later, the Japanese heard their fellow workers discussing the problem of the school. They were very angry when they learned the solution.

"They would rather enrol a dog in their school than a Japanese boy! It is the worst insult yet!"

On the Tuesday that he overheard Stan Rowe taking the phone call about the inspector's visit, Kenta Nakano hurried home. As he turned off the path to follow the stream to their house, he heard music. He stopped to listen. His wife and son were practising. Yuko had brought her violin with her when she came from Japan to marry him. When Shigi was old enough, she encouraged him to join the school band. He was given a flute, which he loved. Soon he was a good player. The music pleased Kenta. Suddenly he scowled and walked on quickly. His son was a fine boy. An obedient son. A good scholar. A musician. Why was he not allowed to go to school with white children? It would be a good thing if that inspector did close the school! See how the white people liked having no way to educate their children.

His frown changed to a smile when he saw little Yumi in the vegetable garden. Wearing a braided straw hat, she was carefully cutting out weeds in a row of beets with the small hoe that Tommy Moriyama had made for her. He stopped to admire her work. But, as he turned away, the scowl returned to his face. Soon she would be old enough for school, too.

When his wife saw his stormy face, she stopped playing. The flute notes also died away.

"What is the matter?" asked Yuko.

He told them the news.

"This inspector will close the school if he finds out about the dog. They do not want that."

Shigi leapt to his feet. "It is my chance," he said, brandishing the flute like a sword. "I will go to school. I will be the tenth pupil. They will have to take me!"

So, dressed in his best clothes, Shigi hurried to the schoolhouse. He crept up on the porch and heard the inspector ask for Shaggy.

Stepping forward, he said boldly, "I am Shigi."

He didn't feel bold. His legs were trembling and his damp palms were staining the books he held clasped to his chest. The children turned to stare at him. One boy was glaring fiercely, but the girl nearest the door seemed pleased to see him. She pointed to the desk beside her. He stood there waiting for permission to sit down. The young woman teacher looked startled, but she didn't challenge him. Was he going to get away with it?

The man scolded him for being late. When he said, "Shaggy Fields," Shigi hesitated only a moment before correcting him. If he was going to attend this school, it would be under his own name.

When the inspector added his name to the roll, Shigi collapsed on to the seat. The girl beside him secretly showed him her arithmetic text. Luckily, he had done that page a week ago with his mother. He opened his own notebook and pretended to work, although at that moment he couldn't have added two and two. His mind was whirling with excitement.

As soon as Mr. Fallis left, Miss Lewis dismissed the class and hurried out of the room. As the children followed her, they stared at Shigi. He spent a lot of time fastening the strap around his books, hoping the others would all be gone before he stepped out. When he looked up, only the girl at the next desk was still there.

"I'm Trudy Paige," she said. "Miss Lewis has gone to see my mother. She's the school trustee."

"I'm staying!" declared Shigi. "He said I could."

"I heard him," answered Trudy.

Outside, the kids were waiting at the side of the building out of sight of anyone in the camp. Nick Carley stepped forward.

"What did you say your name was?" he demanded.

Shigi could see that this boy was going to be trouble. He remembered his parents' advice. "Be polite. Answer softly. Never provoke them."

"I am Shigi Nakano," he answered quietly.

"Shaggy! That's a dog's name," said Nick with a sneer.

Shigi kept quiet.

Nick came close enough for the Japanese boy to feel his breath.

"You better not show up here tomorrow," he hissed. "We don't want no dirty Japs in our school."

Shigi moved two steps back.

"I will come," he said.

Nick reached out, grabbed Shigi's tie and pulled him forward.

"This is Canada!" he said. "Jap men can't vote and Jap kids can't go to school! Got that?"

Shigi twisted away. His hand was itching to swing the strap on his books and smash this kid's mean face. Instead, he smoothed his tie.

"The inspector said I could go to this school," he answered.

"Yeah? Well, my Dad will say you can't! It's our school and we don't want no dirty Japs."

Shigi turned and walked toward the road.

"You're a coward, too!" taunted Nick. "Dirty Jap coward!"

Shigi went on walking. Suddenly, his feet were hooked out from under him and he was shoved hard. He sprawled on the ground at Nick's feet. He rolled over and glared up at the grinning boy.

"Come on! Get up and fight!" said Nick.

Behind him, Shigi saw the other kids huddled together. The girls and the little ones looked scared. A couple of boys seemed eager to watch a fight. Shigi clenched his fists. He'd like to wipe that grin off Nick Carley's face. He winced. One hand was badly scraped. Suddenly he felt murderous. But getting into a fight on the first day was no way to start out in this new school.

He got up and brushed off his pants. The right knee had a jagged hole in it. He picked up his books and quietly turned toward home.

"Coward!" yelled Nick after him.

Nick turned back to the other kids, threw up his head and smirked in triumph.

"I guess I told him," he said.

Trudy shook her head. "Well, I'll say one thing for you. You sure make your words come true."

"What do you mean?" asked Nick suspiciously.

"You called him a dirty Jap. When he arrived, he was probably the cleanest kid who ever came to this school. He's dirty now, all right."

"He won't be back," said Nick with a smirk.

"Of course he will," answered Trudy. "We need him."

That was all Shigi overheard before the racket of the blacksmith shop drowned out the voices. That's where their neighbour, Tommy Moriyama, worked. Shigi walked quickly past the building to the railroad tracks. He didn't want Tommy to see his torn pants and dusty jacket. On the railway bridge, he paused a moment to look south toward the new truck bridge that the men were building. He was fascinated by the engineering of the structure. Huge timbers were interlaced to make a high trestle. It was going to be very strong, much stronger than this railway bridge, which was getting rickety after years of use. Often he watched the men at work from the shelter of the woods near his home on Black Creek. Now that he was going to school he wouldn't have time for that.

Was he going to school? He walked on, staring down at his scuffed shoes. His mother would be angry when she saw him. Would she say he couldn't go back? After he crossed the footbridge on the creek, he stopped to wash his sore hands. He couldn't do anything about the torn pants.

As he expected, his parents were horrified when they saw him.

"He won't go back there!" said his mother.

"Yes, I must go," said Shigi. "Only one boy attacked me. There is a girl who wants me to go to keep the school open. The rest of them don't care about me. I will manage."

He winced as his mother bathed the cut with iodine.

"What about the teacher?" asked his father.

"She was glad I came. It saved her from being found out."

His father nodded gravely. "Yes, It saved them all. They can keep their school." He nodded again. "Go back. Work hard. Please the teacher. You will survive."

5

Stan Rowe

After Shigi walked quietly away, the kids all ran home to report on their exciting day at school. Trudy lagged behind. She watched the Japanese boy until he disappeared behind the log pile at the sawmill. Then she walked slowly over the bridge. The mountain was already casting its shadow on the road and she shivered. She wasn't cold. And she wasn't really worried about the school closing; people would just have to accept the new boy. So, what was bothering her? She shivered again as she remembered Nick's ugly sneer. She hated violence. Sometimes at the floating camp, some of the loggers would drink too much on a Saturday night. Then they'd fight. She remembered being wakened one night by shouting and then a loud splash outside the bedroom window. Dad ordered her to stay in bed, but she peeked out the window and watched him haul a man out of the water. The sight of his bleeding head and the loud, angry shouts of the logger who had thrown him in, made her sick to her stomach. Why did men and boys want to pound one another? She shivered again as someone yelled somewhere along the street. Not another fight! No. It was just her brother and sister racing one another to the Johnsons. Miss Lewis and Mum must have sent them away.

Trudy walked slower and in a few minutes the teacher came out the front door. She passed Trudy with just a tiny smile. Mum waited for her in the doorway. She put her arm around her daughter and pulled her inside.

"What a day, eh?" she said. "I don't ever want a scare like that again!"

"Will Shigi be allowed to come to school?" asked Trudy.

"Of course! I'm just thankful he turned up and got us off the hook. Whew! I need a cup of tea. Want something?"

Trudy set out a tin of cookies and a glass of lemonade while her mother put another stick of wood in the stove.

"How come we never thought of that Japanese boy?" asked Trudy.

"It never entered my head!" answered her mother. "I've hardly ever seen the family and I've never spoken to them. I didn't even know they could speak English."

"But Dad knows Mr. Nakano."

"Only at work. He doesn't know the family."

Trudy nibbled a cookie. She wasn't going to tattle about the fight, but she had to warn her mother.

"Nick Carley was pretty mean to him," she said.

Mum groaned. "Oh, gosh, I hope there won't be trouble. Bill Carley is death on Japanese."

"Why?" asked Trudy.

Mum shrugged. "I guess he has his reasons."

When he heard about Shigi, Bill Carley did try to ban the Japanese boy, but the other families outvoted him. Miss Lewis was delighted with her new pupil. He was polite and smart and hard-working. Trudy found she had to study hard to keep up with him. She enjoyed the challenge.

Mary quickly developed a grudge against Shigi. Until he came, she and Trudy were always picked as captains of the two sides in the Friday afternoon spelling bees. Now, it was Trudy and Shigi.

One Friday, Shigi won the match for his side by correctly spelling "phenomenon" when Mary missed.

"He thinks he's so smart!" she complained to Trudy as they walked home.

"He is smart," replied Trudy mildly.

"Well, he shouldn't show off! Those people always have to have the best of everything."

"You mean Japanese people?"

"Yeah! They catch the most fish. Cut the most trees. Grow the best gardens. Always showing off!"

"Have you seen their garden?" asked Trudy, in surprise.

"No, of course not. I'm not allowed to go down there. My Dad told us. He saw it from the spar tree when he was re-rigging."

Shigi never stayed around to play after school. Trudy knew nothing about him except that he was good at school-work. This news about the garden was the first she had ever heard about his home. Who worked in the garden? Shigi? His mother? The little sister? And what did they grow? Something strange and Japanese? The soil here was not suitable for much except trees. Mum had a few flowers in tubs, but she didn't try to grow vegetables as she had at the old Camp.

"Where do they get the dirt?" she wondered.

"Dad says they bring in bags of seaweed for fertilizer," Mary answered.

"Smart!" said Trudy.

"Greedy!" said Mary.

Trudy kept quiet. There was no point in quarrelling with her best friend over something she knew nothing about. She wished she did know more about the Japanese people. Was their house like all the others in this camp? What did they eat? At home, did they wear kimonos like the people in the picture in the geography book? Mary wasn't the least bit interested. She was glad that Shigi had come to school and kept it open. That was all she cared about him.

Mary and Nick had another grievance against the Japanese boy. They complained to the teacher that he always made faces during God Save The King. Trudy said nothing, but she secretly sided with Shigi. Even though she was not musical, she realized that the daily singing was terrible. Miss Lewis had a tuning fork which started them off on the right note but she couldn't carry a tune and neither could many of the pupils. Trudy was often shaking with inward laughter by the time they sat down to begin work. No wonder Shigi grimaced.

One morning, he brought a small black case to school. Inside was a silver flute. He asked the teacher if he could play for the anthem.

"That would be wonderful," she said.

From then on, he brought the flute every day.

Another morning, Stan Rowe was passing the school and heard the music. That night, he was at the Paiges' house to listen to the radio. He came once a week to play cards and listen to Mart Kenney and His Western Gentlemen from the Alexandra Ballroom in Vancouver. Stan knew one of the men in the band. They had played together in a jazz band in the city when there was lots of work for musicians. Stan played the saxophone and was very, very good. Then the Depression worsened. Not many people could afford to eat out any more so hotels and restaurants closed down. There were few opportunities for a saxophone player. Then Stan lost his daytime job in an accounting office. He ended up back where he had started life — in a logging camp.

He still played. Because not everyone in the bunkhouse

appreciated his sessions on the saxophone, he practised outdoors on the railway bridge in fine weather. The blacksmith shop after hours was a good place on rainy days or dark evenings. He often played at the Paiges' house.

"I didn't know your teacher played the flute," he said that evening.

"She doesn't," answered Muriel. "It was Shigi."

"Really? It sounded great."

"I like the sax better," said Karl.

Stan laughed. "So do I! But he's good. I wonder where he learned?"

"He played in the school band at Storm Inlet," answered Trudy. "Kids could learn any instrument they wanted to."

She had found this out one day after school when she walked with Shigi as far as the railway bridge. She was protecting him from Nick and Al Johnson. That day, Trudy and Shigi had been on clean-up duty. When they finished sweeping the floor, they stored the broom and dustpan on the porch. As they came down the steps, Nick stuck out his foot to trip Shigi. Al was poised to grab the flute case.

But Shigi was alert. He stumbled but didn't fall and he kept a tight hold on the case.

Trudy saw what was happening and her temper flared. She knew the silver flute was valuable and she could tell from the way he handled it that it was very precious to Shigi. What right had those two bullies to touch it?

"Leave him alone," she yelled.

"Says who?" asked Nick.

"Says me!" Trudy answered. She turned to Al. "Does your mother know you're a thief?"

"We weren't stealing it! We were just going to . . ." Al looked at Nick and hesitated.

"What?" demanded Trudy.

"Throw it in the river where it belongs!" answered Nick.

"Scram! Or I'll call the teacher," said Trudy.

"Jap lover!" taunted Nick.

Shigi had already walked away. Trudy joined him. For a few minutes they didn't speak.

At last Trudy asked. "Are you going to leave the flute at home after this?"

"No!" answered Shigi. "If I do, they've won."

His voice was quiet, but Trudy could hear the bitterness behind the words.

She wondered again why some people hated the Japanese. No one had explained to her satisfaction why these people were treated as outcasts. When she asked, grown-ups just said, "They're different." "They keep to themselves." "They stick together." None of these answers satisfied Trudy.

Later, she was glad when Shigi told her that Stan Rowe had visited his family in their home. She was jealous, too. Stan was an adult and could go wherever he wanted. His music made him a welcome guest. The Nakanos would never invite her to visit, and her parents would never let her go without an invitation.

"Stan brought his saxophone and played for us," Shigi told Trudy. "I used to hear him on the bridge sometimes. I wished I could play with him. Well, we did play duets last night. It was fun."

Perhaps Stan would tell her about Shigi's family and the other Japanese men so that she'd understand the prejudice against them. When she asked him, her friend said there was nothing unusual about the family.

"People are just jealous of any success," he told Trudy. "Nick Carley's probably tone deaf. He could never play an instrument, so he hates Shigi, who can."

Trudy was not satisfied with that answer either. Nick had hated Shigi on the first day, before he knew anything about him.

6

Where's Bertie?

There were some warm days in October. Although the temperature began to drop as soon as the sun went down behind the mountain, it was warm enough to play outside during the day.

One Sunday morning Karl was at the Dodds' place playing trucks with Eddie and Bertie. They had the whole back yard to themselves to make roads. Mr. Dodd had gone deer hunting with Mr. Lawson and some of the men from the bunkhouse. They could hear Mr. Johnson splitting kindling two yards over. In the other direction, Mr. Carley and Len were hammering nails as they built a shed. Karl's Dad was listening to the World Series baseball game on the radio while he washed the storm windows and put them on. Next door, Mrs. Lawson's baby cried for a while, but the boys varoomed their engines loud enough to drown her out.

The five girls were playing house on the Paiges' porch. They set out their collection of incomplete doll tea sets, chipped china cups, and a tea pot with a broken spout and no lid. Trudy sent Lorraine and Muriel to pick salal leaves for sandwiches and Frieda and Mary went across the plank road to gather small fir cones for cookies. Trudy put some berries and dried grass in a jam jar for a centrepiece.

"What's the party for?" asked Frieda.

"A wedding," said Muriel.

"No. We've had lots of weddings. Besides, no one wants to be the groom."

"A funeral?" asked Mary.

"No, we did that the last time."

"I know," said Trudy. "A christening."

"What's a christening?" asked Lorraine.

"We went to one in the summer when we were visiting Grandma Holm. You go to church and the Mum and Dad take the baby up to the front and the minister sprinkles water on its head and names it. I'll be the minister."

"I'll be the mother," said Mary.

"You can be the dad, Frieda," said Trudy.

Frieda made a face but she didn't object.

"Muriel, you'll be the baby's auntie and you'll be the baby, Lorraine."

"No, I won't. I'm too big to be a baby." Lorraine crossed her arms and glared.

"Maybe Mrs. Lawson will loan us Baby Jill," said Frieda.

"She won't," said Mary. "She'd think we'd drop her or something."

"How about Bertie?" asked Trudy. "He likes to play with us. I'll go and get him."

Bertie was a willing actor and stood still while Trudy sprinkled water on him from the tea pot. He sat on Mary's lap at the party, but when she wanted to put him to bed on a blanket in the corner of the porch, he objected.

"I'm going home," he said.

"You can't go. The party's not over."

"I have to peepee."

"Use our privy," said Trudy.

She watched him walk around the corner of the house and then turned back to join in the conversation of the guests. They all forgot about him.

While the girls and younger boys were busy, Al and Nick were having a good time at the bunkhouse. Trudy said they thought they were big shots because they were the only kids allowed over there. Sunday was always wash day for the loggers. Two men usually shared a wooden wash tub. One logger shaved a bar of soap into flakes while the other carried pails of hot water. They threw in their long johns, sweaty socks and greasy shirts. Then they pounded the clothes with a log to loosen the dirt. Today, because of the World Series, they wanted to stay close to the cook's radio. So they paid Nick and Al a dime apiece to keep the fire going under the hot water boiler.

Soon the laundry was pegged out to dry on ropes strung between the bunkhouse and other buildings. Everybody listened to the bottom half of the ninth inning of the game. The St. Louis Cardinals won on Dizzy Dean's great pitching.

Inspired by the game, a few men crossed the tracks to the new road and tossed a ball around. They had all played baseball in other places, but there was no space big enough for a real game in Mellor's Camp. Al and Nick watched.

"Gee, Pete, you're as good as Dizzy Dean," said Nick. "Can you show me how to pitch?"

One of the men laughed. "Come on, Kid! Pete's the best pitcher on the coast. You can't learn that in a day."

"I just wanted to try," said Nick.

Pete beckoned him over. Someone else gave Al a mitt. They were playing ball with the loggers. What a perfect day.

❧

Just before noon, Mrs. Dodd stuck her head out of the window.

"Time to get washed up for lunch, boys," she said. "Where's Bertie?"

"He went to play with Trudy," Eddie answered.

"Tell him to come home, will you, Karl?"

"Okay, Mrs. Dodd."

The girls were still on the porch. Karl gave them Mrs. Dodd's message and went around to see his Dad.

A few minutes later, Mrs. Dodd stood on her porch and shouted for Bertie. She sounded mad.

She strode down the street.

"Girls, where's Bertie?"

"He went home, Mrs. Dodd," answered Trudy.

"When?"

"Uh, I don't know. A long time ago, I guess." Trudy looked at the other girls who nodded.

"He needed to peepee," said Lorraine.

"He wouldn't take this long," said Mary.

"Maybe he went to see Mrs. Sutton. She gives him cookies," Frieda said.

"We'll find him for you," said Trudy.

The girls scattered and checked all the houses. After Mrs. Sutton told them she hadn't seen Bertie, Trudy and Mary knocked on Miss Lewis' door. The teacher was writing a letter.

"Did Bertie come here, Miss Lewis?"

"No. Why?"

"We can't find him," said Trudy.

"Oh dear. Well, I've been sitting right here all morning marking notebooks and writing letters. I haven't seen him." She saw the worried look on Trudy's face. "Could he have gone to school?"

"He's not supposed to cross the bridge by himself," Mary said.

"Still, let's go and look."

Shaggy peered out from under the porch as the three of them climbed the steps.

"Hey, Shaggy," said Trudy, "is Bertie down there with you?" She bent over and looked. No Bertie. He wasn't in the school either. Nor anywhere on the grounds.

"Is he playing hide and seek?" asked Miss Lewis.

"He wouldn't play this long when no one was looking for him," answered Trudy. "It must be about an hour since anyone saw him."

"Oh dear," said the teacher.

The three of them frowned at one another. They could hear shouts of "Bertie!" from the street. Followed by Shaggy, they hurried back to the Dodd house.

By this time, all the women were there. When she saw them without Bertie, Mrs. Dodd looked ready to cry.

"Have you checked the big house?" asked Mrs. Sutton. "I know Mr. Mellor is away for the weekend in Vancouver. And we saw the boys leave in a car early this morning, but they probably didn't lock up."

"He's not supposed to cross the bridge," said Mrs. Dodd. "Those are his limits — the two bridges."

"Well, but . . ." said Mrs. Sutton.

"I'll go look," said Mrs. Paige. "Muriel can come with me. The rest of you check the houses again. He could be hiding for fun. Try under the beds," she called back as she strode off to catch up to Muriel.

They crossed the bridge together, making the planks

rattle. Twenty minutes later, subdued and rather frightened, they almost tiptoed back over the bridge. They had searched the house, the out buildings and the edge of the woods without success.

The fathers, who had not taken the fuss seriously at first, had now joined the search for the lost boy. They had been across the plank road and along the river path. Tom Paige looked at his wife as she came up to the group gathered around Mrs. Dodd. She shook her head.

"Okay," said Tom. "He's not around here, that's for sure. It will start to get dark in another hour. We've got to organize a proper search. Get the men at the bunkhouse to help and cover the woods and the . . ." He saw the last of the colour drain from Mrs. Dodd's face. ". . . buildings on the other side."

"The river!" moaned Mrs. Dodd. "You were going to say the river!"

"We'll find him," said Tom. "Come on, men, let's go to the bunkhouse."

"Mellor's away," said Mr. Johnson.

"Stan Rowe will organize it," answered Tom, striding toward the bridge. "Karl, you come with us. You can bring a message back to Mrs. Dodd. Tell her what we're doing."

7

The Search

Mr. Sutton, Mr. Johnson, Mr. Carley and Len searched the blacksmith shop, the sawmill, the engine and its shed. Tom Paige and Karl found Stan. As soon as he understood what had happened, Stan rang the iron triangle outside the cookhouse door.

The cook's angry face appeared. "What do you think you're doing? We're not ready."

"Trouble," said Stan. "Get everyone out here."

A large crowd gathered. Stan explained about the lost child.

"The kid's been gone about two hours now. The families are sure he's nowhere on the street. So we need to search the woods."

"The river?" whispered one man who had a little son of his own in Duncan.

"We don't think so," answered Tom Paige. "There's no slip marks on the bank or anything like that."

"Still, we'd better get a boat out there," said Stan. "Dunc, is your rowboat okay?" Dunc nodded. "Take a couple of men with you. Nick could go, he's light. The rest of you pair up and we'll assign sections. He may have wandered into the woods and got lost."

Carley interrupted. "Maybe the Japs got him."

Stan looked at him in disgust. "Rot!" he said. "They've got kids of their own."

"Yeah, well maybe he went down there," Carley muttered.

"I'll go and see," said Tom. "Al can come with me. We'll ask them to hunt along Black Creek."

"You cooks stay here," said Stan. "If it's a long search, the men will get hungry."

"Can't be long," said Mr. Sutton. "It'll be dark soon."

"Right," answered Stan. "So take flashlights. And wear your work boots."

"I'll get the dogs and my rifle," said Bruiser Olds.

"What for? That'll only scare him."

"Bears," said Bruiser.

Al gasped and looked with scared eyes at his pale-faced Dad.

"Oh God," whispered Stan. "Yeah, okay. Now, remember,

the rest of you, he's only a little guy — just five years old. He could be behind even a small tree or hidden in the underbrush. One last thing, we'll need a signal. Where's that whistle punk? Carley?"

"Right here," answered Len.

"Go and get steam up in your whistle. Give us two long toots if he's found. And four short toots to call everybody in to report. You all got that? Okay. Now, stick with your partner. If you find him, one of you bring him back here and the other go to the whistle station and tell Len to give the signal."

Within five minutes, only Stan and Karl remained at the bunkhouse.

"Karl, go back and tell Mrs. Dodd we've got about thirty men out there. Tell her about the signals. You remember them?"

"Two long when they find him and four toots to come back."

"Then you come back here. I might need you for another message. I'll be in the first aid room."

Karl knew that Stan expected Bertie to be hurt, but he didn't want to think about that. He ran like a deer.

When Tom Paige and Al neared the Nakano house, three men and Shigi stood on the pathway. One of the men had cards in his hand. They had been playing poker.

"We heard all the noise," said Ken Nakano. "What's up?"

Tom told them about the missing boy. "Did he come over here?"

They shook their heads.

"Will you hunt along Black Creek for him?"

"Of course. Of course."

They divided up and started immediately.

There was nothing that Mrs. Dodd and her neighbours could do but wait. If they went into the woods, they would just confuse the searchers. They had hunted through every inch of the street. Just sitting and waiting was too hard. Leaving Eddie with Mrs. Lawson and the baby, Mrs. Dodd roamed up and down the river path and through all the back yards. Off and on the other women and children joined her. Mrs. Sutton stayed home making tea and piles of sandwiches.

Trudy sat alone on the Suttons' porch, nibbling one of the sandwiches and thinking about Bertie. Just last night she had been babysitting with him and Eddie while their parents played cards at the Lawsons' house. She had read him his favourite story book, *The Three Billy Goats Gruff*. He liked to be the troll and say, "Who's that walking over my bridge?"

The bridge!

Trudy froze with the sandwich halfway to her mouth.

Could Bertie be playing troll?

Not under the big bridge. They had all looked there and she had seen the rowboat pass back and forth under it. What about the foot bridge to the Mellors' house?

She jumped up but before she called out she had another thought. It would be cruel to get his mother's hopes up, if Bertie weren't there.

Quietly she went into her own house and got a flashlight. Shaggy was on the porch when she came out and suddenly she wanted company. Although she felt like running, she forced herself to walk slowly. She didn't need a string of girls with her, if she were wrong. It was getting cold now. She shivered.

The bridge was only four feet above the stream. Earlier her Dad had climbed down the bank and peered underneath.

Bertie can't be here, she thought as she lay across the bridge and hung her head over the side. It was dark. She turned on the flashlight and directed it at both sides of the bank.

To support the bridge three log posts had been driven into the stream bed on each side. On top of each set of posts a log had been fastened crosswise to hold the planks. Each post was braced by a log placed at an angle. Below the logs a flat board was wedged between the posts and the bank of the stream. Bertie could have hidden behind a log under the board. It was a good place for a troll.

He wasn't there.

Trudy almost cried with disappointment.

Then Shaggy barked.

"What, Shaggy? Have you found him?"

The dog barked again, slid down the bank and went under the bridge.

Trudy stumbled after him.

"Where, Shaggy? Where?"

She flashed her light all around each of the logs. No little boy.

"Shaggy?"

The old dog scrambled up the bank, stuck his nose in the space between the board and the planks, lost his balance and slid down into the water.

Clinging to the log post with one arm, Trudy shone her light into the small space.

There lay Bertie, looking as if he had just wakened from a deep sleep.

Trudy wanted to scream at him. Instead she said, "You have to come home now, Bertie. Your Mum's looking for you."

The hiding place was a tight fit and Trudy had to help Bertie out.

"What were you doing in there, anyway?" she asked.

"I'm a troll," said Bertie.

"Didn't you hear everyone calling you?"

Bertie giggled. "I knew someone would come here. I was going to scare them."

Trudy boosted him up to the road. "Didn't you hear my Mum cross the bridge?"

"Uh, huh. I heard two people. I was going to say 'Who's that walking on my bridge,' when they came back. But they took too long. I fell asleep."

As Trudy dragged him along, she shouted "Mum! Mrs. Dodd! Mum! Mrs. Dodd!"

All the women and girls came running. Mrs. Dodd grabbed Bertie and hugged and scolded him alternately.

"Good girl, Trudy," said her Mum. "You found him!"

"Shaggy found him," said Trudy.

The girls swarmed all over the wet dog.

"Where was he?" asked many voices.

"Wait," said Mrs. Paige. "Someone — you, Mary, you're the fastest — run and tell Stan."

Mary was gone before she finished speaking.

They were all gathered in Mrs. Sutton's kitchen wolfing down salmon sandwiches and tea when they heard the welcome sound of two long, triumphant toots on the steam whistle.

8
The Concert

For the next few days everybody talked about the search for Bertie. Then life in the camp settled back into routine. Trudy went to school, played with her friends and enjoyed Stan Rowe's weekly visit with her family.

One evening, Stan praised Mrs. Nakano's skill on the violin.

"We should get up a concert so everyone can hear her and Shigi," he said one day at the Paiges'.

"Good idea!" said Mum. "You could play the sax. And there's Pete's accordion."

"There's at least two mouth organs in the bunkhouse," said Stan.

"Yeah! I like them!" said Karl.

"Maybe the kids could do something," said Mum. "We could ask Miss Lewis."

"Not sing!" yelled Trudy and Muriel together.

"Okay," laughed Mum. "How about a spelling bee?"

Half an hour later, they had a whole evening of fun planned for the schoolhouse on the first Saturday in December.

Trudy was a bit worried.

"What if some people don't like us having Shigi and his mother in the concert?" she asked.

"They can stay home!" answered her mother. "But they won't. Who in his right mind would want to miss the first ever concert in the Mellor Schoolhouse?"

On the day of the concert frost sparkled on the porch steps and the plank road. Grey clouds threatened snow. In spite of that, almost everyone came. Mr. Mellor was there, sitting on the teacher's chair. All the families were there and most of the men from the bunkhouse. People brought their kitchen chairs. The loggers brought the benches from the cookhouse. There wasn't room for everyone to sit down. Many of the men stood at the back and sides of the room and wandered out and in during the evening.

The Japanese were all there, sitting in a row. Trudy was hoping that Mrs. Nakano and her little girl would be wearing kimonos. They weren't. They wore dresses like everybody else. Yumi's was of pink organdy with frills on the collar and hem. She looked like a little doll with her straight black hair and dark eyes as she sat on her father's lap and peeked shyly over his arm.

Trudy smiled and wriggled her fingers at her. The little girl almost smiled then suddenly looked frightened and tucked her face in the crook of her father's elbow. Mr. Nakano frowned and turned his head away. Trudy stared at his rigid back. What had she done? Then she heard a giggle behind her and turned to see Nick using his fingers to make his eyes slanted. Al copied him and some of the men standing near them laughed.

"Stop that!" hissed Trudy, just as Miss Lewis called everyone to order and welcomed them. Stan introduced the musicians who played a lively *Roll Out The Barrel* on saxophone, flute, accordion and two harmonicas. It got a footstomping reception from the loggers' boots. Then Stan played a medley of jazz tunes on his sax. As always, Trudy watched his fingers. She was fascinated by the way they moved up and down the shaft and hovered over a key like a butterfly deciding where to land. Every day lately she had seen Shigi's fingers do the same thing on the flute. His small hands seemed more suited to music than Stan's work-scarred ones.

Now it was time for Shigi and his mother to perform. Trudy knew that with the teacher there none of the kids would dare to be rude. What about the loggers? As Stan introduced Mrs. Nakano and her son, Trudy sat on her hands, stared at the floor and listened intently. A few people clapped when the two musicians took their places. That was all. Trudy let out her breath and looked up. Even though Shigi's face was blank, she knew he must be scared. She herself was nervous about the spelling bee coming up. How much worse to play an instrument.

Except for the fiddler who played for dances in the old camp, the only violinist Trudy had ever heard was Jack Benny on the radio. His playing was so terrible it was funny. She thought of him as Mrs. Nakano tuned her violin. The squawks and squeaks were the same. Fortunately, she played much better than Jack Benny. Still, Trudy felt that most people were just sitting quietly through it, not enjoying it. Was that because the players were Japanese? Or because they didn't like that kind of music? She was relieved when the short piece was over.

The next number was very popular. Four loggers played a medley of old tunes on harmonicas. While the soloist rattled through *Turkey in the Straw* at a breakneck pace, Karl stood up and stared with his mouth open. During the applause, he pulled his own mouth organ out of his pants pocket and stared at it. Would he ever be able to make those sounds?

While Pete played a polka on the accordion, Trudy grinned at her Mum and Dad whose feet were dancing to the music. Beyond them, she saw Miss Lewis leafing through the speller. Oh, gosh! For a few minutes, she had forgotten about the spelling bee. Just the sax and flute duet and they were on!

She and Mary were the captains since Shigi had decided

that the music was enough for him. To calm herself she concentrated on the duet. Stan and Shigi were both good players and they sounded great together. Maybe they'd play an encore and postpone the spelling bee. No. Stan called Miss Lewis and the children to the front. Eddie Powell was too young to spell, so that left four on each team: Trudy Paige, Al Johnson, Frieda Carley and Lorraine Johnson against Mary Johnson, Nick Carley, Muriel Paige and Karl Paige.

As they stood in two facing lines waiting to begin, Trudy heard Len Carley say, in a low but carrying voice, "Guess the Jap kid can't spell in English."

"Maybe he just can't spell," said the young man next to him.

Miss Lewis had her back to the audience. Only the children saw her face turn white. She took a deep breath. Then she forced a smile and said, "Do your best, everyone." At first, she called easy words so that the youngest would have a chance. Karl was the first one out. Lorraine lasted one more round. Now the words got harder. Nick went down, then Frieda. The audience clapped after each success. At last, Al misspelled *fortunately*. That left Trudy against Mary and Muriel. They went on until Miss Lewis closed the book with a snap.

"We'll have to declare a tie," she said. "We've used up all the words in the speller."

"Try some logging words," suggested Mr. Mellor.

"Good idea," she answered. "Would you call one? It's Muriel's turn."

Mr. Mellor winked at the girl. "High rigger," he said.

Muriel grinned back at him. Their grandfather, Karl Holm, was the most famous high rigger on the coast. Even though he'd been retired for years, loggers everywhere still talked about the speed with which he could climb up a high tree, lop off the top and rig the spar with ropes and pulleys. Once he had even stood on the new cut and danced a jig way up in the sky.

"High rigger," she repeated. "Two words. High *high*, rigger *riger*." As soon as she finished, she knew she'd made a mistake. She didn't need the great groan from the audience to tell her. Her face turned beet red and she ran to her father and hid her blushes in his coat.

Trudy felt very sorry for her sister. Should she make a mistake so Muriel wouldn't feel so bad? She couldn't. If rigger didn't have one g it had two. She spelled it correctly.

Mr. Mellor called out more words until Mary fumbled on *chokerman* and Trudy got it right. Thank goodness, since that was their father's job. It would be a terrible disgrace if two Paiges missed on logging words. Then she spelled *planing mill* correctly and her team was declared the winner. Whew! It was over! She plopped in to the seat next to Mum, who gave her a one-armed hug.

Dad said, "Atta girl" and grinned.

Now she could relax and listen to Mrs. Nakano's solo.

Stan announced that she was going to play *Sonata for Violin* by Haydn.

"I'm going hiding myself," said a young logger and stomped out. Several others followed him to the porch where Trudy could hear them talking and laughing until Mr. Mellor joined them.

The piece began with a quiet, pretty melody. Trudy smiled to herself. It was going to be okay. Then the music changed. Mrs. Nakano closed her eyes and swayed as her arm pushed the bow faster and faster across the strings. Nick clapped his hands over his ears. Al copied him. Mrs. Johnson pulled his hands away and frowned at Mary who was giggling with Frieda. Muriel covered her mouth with her hands and Karl made a face as if he smelled something bad. Trudy looked at her parents. Dad was staring at the floor and Mum had a blank look on her face as she gazed steadily at the violinist. Trudy could feel laughter bubbling up inside herself, until she caught sight of Shigi. He was sitting straight and still beside his father. Both of them were clearly aware of the feeling in the room. She sobered instantly. Mrs. Nakano was completely absorbed in her music. Only one person seemed to appreciate it. Looking past the row of Japanese men, Trudy saw that young Mrs. Lawson was as rapt as the musician. You could tell she thought the sonata was beautiful. Trudy didn't. To her it sounded like sharpening a saw. She only controlled the giggles by staring at Shigi.

Suddenly, a voice from the doorway called, "Hasn't she got that tree down yet?"

Many people laughed. Mrs. Nakano paled. She paused for a split second before continuing.

At the end, Trudy, Mrs. Lawson and Stan clapped the loudest. A few others applauded politely. The violinist took one short bow and then quickly sat down beside her husband. She took her daughter on to her lap. Trudy saw that her hand was trembling on the child's back. She wished that she was brave enough to go over and say something to the woman or to Shigi. If only he would look at her, so that she could smile at him. He was sitting with his head down listening to his father. Mr. Nakano had his hand under Shigi's elbow and seemed to be trying to force him to stand up. He was probably telling him to go and join Stan, Pete and the harmonica players for the final number. Why should he? If anyone had insulted Trudy's Mum like that, she sure wouldn't play for them.

Stan called, "Come on, Shigi, we need you."

He played a few notes that seemed to echo his words. Shigi looked up. Stan smiled and beckoned with his chin. Shigi picked up his flute and walked, wooden-faced, to the front.

The finale was rousing and fast. The audience demanded an encore. After that, Stan spoke.

"Thanks for coming," he said. "But don't go away yet. Just give the women a few minutes to set out the food and come back and eat up. Maybe we'll have a dance afterwards, if anybody's interested."

"Whoo-ee!"

"You bet!"

Most of the fathers went home to get pots of coffee which were keeping hot on the kitchen stoves. Trudy helped her mother lift the tea towels off plates of sandwiches and cakes. She hid Mum's spicy raisin cake with caramel icing behind a pile of mugs. She was going to serve it personally to the Nakano family. When she turned around, there were no Japanese in the room.

"Where's Shigi?" she asked Mary.

"They all skedaddled," answered her friend.

"Why?" asked Trudy, stunned.

Mary shrugged. "Maybe they eat different food." She giggled. "They sure play different music. Squeak! Squawk!"

Behind her, Al pretended to play a violin. He made weird noises in his throat. People waiting in the food line laughed. Karl imitated Al. Trudy grabbed her brother by the shoulders and shook him.

"Stop that!" she ordered.

She really wanted everyone to stop laughing at Mrs. Nakano, but she couldn't shake them all. And she really couldn't have explained just how she felt. Somehow, she knew that it was wrong to make fun of people because they were different. She looked around. No one else seemed to care that the Japanese had left. They were all having a great time, eating and laughing and telling stories.

She retrieved her mother's cake and carried it over to Stan who was standing by himself sorting out sheet music.

"Ah, my favourite cake," he said. "Thanks, Trudy, you're a real pal. Smart, too," he added with his mouth full. "I could never spell."

"And I can't play the sax," she replied.

Trudy nibbled at a piece of cake to keep him company.

"Stan," she said, "why did Shigi and the others leave?"

"That's the way they are," he answered. "They keep to themselves."

Once again, Trudy was not satisfied with that answer. She wanted to force Stan to explain. Before she could speak, Pete came along to ask what tunes they would play for dancing and Stan turned to him.

In a few minutes a space in the middle of the room was cleared. Tom and Ellie Paige were the first on the floor. They loved to dance and usually their daughter loved to watch them. Tonight she couldn't get into the party mood. She had one polka with her Dad and a schottische with the cookee from the bunkhouse.

After the second dance, she overheard Mrs. Dodd telling her husband that she was going to take little Bertie home. He couldn't settle down to sleep in the noisy room. Trudy could see that she was very disappointed to be missing the fun.

"I'll stay with him, Mrs. Dodd," she said.

The woman's face lit up. "Really, Trudy? Oh, no! I couldn't let you. You want to dance, too."

"No, I don't," said Trudy. "Really, Mrs. Dodd. It's too noisy in here."

Bertie and Eddie were both willing to go with Trudy and soon she was sitting quietly on the couch in the Dodds' living room. The boys were asleep. She could hear the music from the school house and it made her feel both sad and mad. She had expected to have a lot of fun at the concert and dance, but it had all been spoiled for her. She was mad at Stan for ever suggesting the concert. He should have known what would happen. And at her mother who let the Japanese leave without trying to stop them. And at Mary and Al and Nick for the way they mocked Shigi and his mother. And at the adults who laughed with them. And what about herself? Would she have tried to stop Shigi if she'd seen him leaving? She wasn't sure.

It was so puzzling. What was it about the Japanese that made people hate them? She curled up in a corner of the couch and tucked an afghan around her. She wished she knew the Nakano family better. Maybe then she'd understand.

She was half asleep when the Dodds came home at midnight.

"It's snowing," said Mrs. Dodd, stamping her feet.

"Good," said Trudy, sleepily.

"Depends on how you look at it," Mr. Dodd said. "The boss will probably close down. No work, no pay."

9

Invitation to Vancouver

By morning the snow was eight inches deep. Mr. Mellor decided to shut down the camp for a month. The exodus from the bunkhouse began after lunch on Sunday and by that evening all the loggers had left. Some went out by speeder on the rails and some by crummy on the road. From Cowichan Lake they made their way to Nanaimo, Victoria or Vancouver to spend their wages.

Trudy didn't see the Japanese leave. Her father told her he had seen them drive away early Monday morning in an old pickup with Tommy Moriyama at the wheel and Mrs. Nakano and Yumi beside him in the cab. Shigi and the other men rode in the back.

"Where were they going?" asked Muriel.

"Probably to Vancouver," answered Trudy. "There's a part that's called Little Tokyo."

"Powell Street, near the waterfront," added her father. "It used to be filled with marine supply stores and stuff like that. It's all Japanese now."

Trudy nodded. "Shigi told me they go there every year to visit friends."

She wondered how the Japanese celebrated Christmas. They probably didn't go to church, but did the children get presents? She was sorry she didn't have a chance to speak to Shigi. Yet, what could she have said? If she didn't like what happened at the concert, she should have spoken up then.

The Paiges were going to Milton to stay with Grandma and Grandpa Holm for Christmas. He was going to pick them up at the old camp.

On Monday, Trudy and Muriel helped their mother and the teacher clean up the school and leave it tidy for a month. When Miss Lewis' brother drove in to pick her up after lunch, he complained about the state of the road.

"It's a real mess," he said. "Snow drifts, ice patches, pot holes, and more snow coming, they say. Anybody who doesn't get out today will be stuck here for a month."

Mr. and Mrs. Sutton and two watchmen were staying in the camp, so that just left the Paige family and the speeder-man to go out. After listening to the weather forecast on the radio at suppertime, they decided to play it safe and leave immediately.

It was a spooky trip. The speeder had a roof and side curtains that were rolled down. The family sat on benches with their backs to the curtains while the driver perched on a stool facing forward. Over his shoulder, Trudy could see trees looming up in the headlight and then disappearing. Once Muriel said she saw a bear's eyes. Fred, the speeder-man, laughed.

"Bears are too smart to be out on a night like this. They're all asleep for the winter."

"Maybe it was a cougar," said Karl.

"Nope," said Fred. "It was imagination."

Talking of cougars reminded Trudy of Shaggy, who was once a great cougar hunter. The old dog had been left with Mrs. Sutton, and Trudy missed him already.

It began to snow again. Fred slowed to a crawl. Dad moved up beside him to help keep watch.

Suddenly Dad called, "Look out! Tree down."

Fred swore and pulled on the brake. He jumped down for a closer look.

"Not very big," he said. "We can chop it up and haul it off."

Soon he and Dad were using the axes Fred always carried under the seat. Mum tucked the legs of her slacks into her boots and went to drag away the chopped branches.

"You kids stay put," she ordered. "The snow's deep. You'd get soaked."

The three of them watched anxiously. It was bitter cold in the speeder. How long would they be held up? The headlight made huge shadows of the three workers on the near-by trees. They looked like grotesque giants. Trudy imagined the sound she heard was the giants grunting. Then she realized that it was a tree moaning and cracking. She snatched up the side curtain and peered upward. The top of a fir was about to fall on the speeder! No use yelling for Fred. The tree would hit before he could board. She shoved Muriel and Karl to the front of the cab, grabbed the operating lever and pushed. The speeder moved forward. Fred and Dad looked up in surprise. They leaped off the track just as the fir crashed behind the speeder. Fred swore. Mum screamed. Trudy put on the brake. Then she leaned weakly against the metal post until Dad gathered her in his arms. Mum was hugging the other two kids. Fred finished clearing the track in front and climbed back in.

"Let's get out of here!" he said.

At the end of the line in the old camp Karl was the first to jump down from the speeder.

"There's Grandpa!" he shouted.

Karl Holm picked him up and lifted him over his head.

"Whew! Either you've grown or I'm getting weak!" he said. "Come on, everyone. Pile in. I brought the pickup."

The truck veered and slithered on the slippery road. Once it went into the ditch. With Mum at the wheel while Dad and Grandpa pushed, they drove it out again. Everyone was exhausted when they finally arrived in Grandma's kitchen. It was warm, there were cinnamon buns on the table, and a pot of cocoa bubbled on the stove.

It was a good start to a happy holiday. From other visits, the Paiges knew lots of town kids. As long as the snow lasted they all built snowmen, snow dogs and forts. There were parties with board games, cards, music and great story-telling. Many of the stories were about Karl Holm's days as a high rigger. These were young Karl's favourites. He was very proud of his grandfather.

"Why did you quit, Grandpa?" he asked.

"Lost my nerve." Grandpa snapped his fingers. "Just like that. Yep. One day I had all my gear on: cleats, safety belt, axe in my belt, spikes, rope. It was a hundred-foot tree. I stood at the base and looked up and up and up. Nope, I thought, I'm not going up there. I dropped all my gear on the spot and made for the bunkhouse. Packed up and hitched a ride on the first boat leaving the dock. Ended up here and got a job in the mill."

"Thank goodness," said Grandma. "I like him on the ground where it's safe."

That led to more stories about accidents in the woods and heroic rescues. There were also fishing stories and tales about wild animals. Trudy had heard many of them before. She loved them all the same.

On Christmas Eve there was a phone call for Mum from Vancouver.

Mrs. Mellor was on the line.

When she hung up, Mum turned to Trudy. "The Mellor

girls want you to go to Vancouver for a week after New Year's. Their Dad and the boys will be away, so there will be room for you."

Trudy gasped. "Really? Just me? Can I go?"

"We'll talk to your father when he comes in."

"Oh, please, Mum!"

"We'll see what Dad says."

Trudy had to wait. She had been to the big city only once before. When she was eight years old, Grandma Paige took her there to have her teeth fixed. That hadn't been much fun. They had seen a movie and done some shopping in the department stores. What she remembered most, though, was the pain and the smell of the dentist's office. It would be great to go just for a visit, especially with the Mellor girls. Anne had written twice. She was homesick for the woods, but she did like some things about city life. Movies, for instance. And streetcars.

"You can go all over the city for a nickel," she wrote. "It's like going on an adventure, only safer because you can stay on the car."

When Dad heard about the invitation, he phoned one of his friends who ran a freight and passenger service between Vancouver and towns on the coast of Vancouver Island. On January 2nd he would be at the town of Maple Bay at the mouth of the Cowichan River.

"Jack says he'll keep her on board till the Mellors come for her, so that's okay."

"And Mr. Mellor will bring her right back to camp on the 10th," added Mum. "So I guess she can go."

"Hurray," yelled Trudy.

Christmas Day was so busy with presents and the huge family dinner party that Trudy didn't have time to think about Vancouver. She found it hard to wait through the next few days. Sometimes she wished she wasn't going. It would be her first time away from home without a relative. Would she be very homesick?

It was pitch black and pouring rain when she and Dad set off in Grandpa's car for Maple Bay. She had been too excited to eat a proper breakfast, so Grandma added an orange and another sandwich to the lunch box she'd prepared.

"You're not feeding a logger," protested Dad.

"The boat may be delayed," said Grandma firmly. "She might need it."

There were four other passengers from Maple Bay: a young woman taking her mother to the city hospital and two loggers. The sea was rough and the two women felt sick as soon as the *Myrna May* left the dock. The men stayed on deck for two more stops. When the boat left the coast and headed across the strait, all the passengers, except Trudy, went into the saloon. Captain Jack had loaned her a yellow oilskin and sou'wester to protect her good coat and dress. She leaned against the railing and watched the shoreline lighten as day came. Gulls, cranes and herons didn't seem to mind the rain any more than she did. In the little settlements a few houses had lights on, but the only people to be seen were one or two who had business with the boat.

Out in the strait, there was nothing to see but waves and a few gulls overhead. Trudy went inside. The sea air had made her hungry. Bracing herself against the door jamb, she took off her slicker. Then she used the railing along the wall to pull herself into the corner where the luggage was stowed. She found her lunch box and staggered over to one end of the long table. Most of the passengers were lying on the benches against the wall, but two men were playing cards at the table.

The red haired one looked at Trudy's sandwiches, cookies and fruit.

"You're not going to eat that, are you?" he asked.

"Yes," she answered. "Do you want some? There's plenty."

"No thanks!"

He turned his back on her.

"You must have a strong stomach, kid," said the other man.

Trudy looked around. Everyone did look pretty sick. She was hungry, though. She ate two sandwiches and listened to the men talk as they played.

"You hear about the trouble up at Crown Point?" asked the redhead.

"Davies' camp? No. What happened."

"Big fight. White men against East Indians."

As they continued to slap down cards, he described the fight in detail as he'd heard it from an eye-witness. Two men hospitalized; many minor injuries; work stopped for several days. Trudy shuddered as she listened.

"Davies is crazy," said the taller man. "Bad enough expecting white men to work alongside Hindoos. He puts them in the same bunkhouse! Employment Office offered me a job there once." He shuffled the cards and slapped the deck angrily down on the table. "Not me! I wasn't living with no Hindoos!" He dealt swiftly. "I hate their guts! Dirty, brown scum!"

Trudy's stomach lurched. The hatred in the man's voice made her tremble with fright. She dropped the last cookie back into the lunch box, jumped up and grabbed her coat.

Both men looked up at her and grinned.

"I told you, kid," said the tall one. "You shouldn't have tried to eat."

Trudy wanted to shout at him, "It's not the food that's making me sick! It's you!"

Then he might say ugly things to her and she really would up-chuck her lunch. With trembling hands she pulled on her slicker and stumbled out onto the deck. Leaning on the rail, she stared unseeing at the waves. The memory of how Mrs. Nakano had been treated at the concert came back. She had felt the same hatred there, but at least at Mellor's Camp there was no fighting. Then she remembered how Nick had greeted Shigi on the first day he appeared at school. There would have been a fight, if the Japanese boy had retaliated. Once again she asked herself why people hated one another.

Captain Jack stuck his head out of the wheelhouse. "Hop up here, Trudy. Get a good view of Vancouver Harbour as we come in."

Glad to escape her gloomy thoughts, Trudy stepped over the sill into the small room with windows on all sides. From there, she could see both the north and south shores covered in forest.

"Stanley Park just ahead," said Captain Jack after a few more minutes. "Been to the zoo there?"

"No."

"Not the best time of year to see it," said the captain. "Still, there's lots of other things to do in the city."

Now they were sailing past streets of big buildings stretching back up the hill from the waterfront. The city was huge. A person could get lost there. When they were close enough to see people on the streets, she wondered whether everyone would realize she was just in from the woods. Grandma had paid for a haircut at the Beauty Salon in Milton. Grandpa said it made her look like a real city slicker, but she doubted that it would be enough to make her fit in. She sighed deeply.

"Getting excited?" asked the captain.

She nodded.

"That's our dock ahead. It will be almost dark by the

time we tie up so if there's no one to meet you, stay on board. Okay?"

"Okay," answered Trudy, hoping fervently that the Mellors would be there.

Five minutes later, she yelled, "I see them! Under that light! Anne and Dave."

Anne waved with both arms over her head. Trudy answered the same way. When she stepped on to the dock, she staggered.

Dave, reaching for her bag, laughed. "You've still got your sea legs," he said.

Anne gave her a hug. "I'm so glad you came!"

"Me too," answered Trudy.

"We're going to go shopping and to a movie and I got tons of Christmas presents to show you and . . ."

"Tell her on the streetcar," said Dave. "We're already late for supper. I'm starving!"

The two girls linked arms and giggled. It was great to be together again.

10

Vancouver

At ten o'clock that night, Helen threatened to kick her sister and Trudy out of bed unless they stopped talking and giggling. The three girls were sleeping in Helen's bed because Dave was using Anne's room. He would be leaving in the morning to join his brother in Seattle for a week to look at truck logging operations.

"You can talk all night tomorrow when you're in your own bed," said Helen. "I've got school in the morning and I need my sleep. So shut up!"

Anne fell asleep first. Trudy found it harder to settle down. It had been a long and exciting day. She wasn't sure yet whether coming to the city was a good idea. Anne seemed just the same, Mrs. Mellor was as kind as ever, but Helen acted like a stuck-up high school girl.

Next morning, the Mellor girls had to go to school. At breakfast, Anne asked Trudy if she wanted to walk with her to Macdonald Elementary School.

"How will I get home?" asked Trudy.

Helen laughed. "It's only three blocks. You can't get lost."

"You did the first day," retorted Anne.

Helen glowered at her. "Templeton School is farther away. Besides, it was foggy and I couldn't see the mountains. It's a big building," she explained to Trudy. "I came out a different door on to a different street. I wasn't really lost."

"Huh!" said Anne.

"Get on with your breakfast, you two," said their mother. "You'll be late. I'll take Trudy with me to shop on Hastings Street. We'll go past the school and the church. She'll see all the neighbourhood sights." As Anne opened the back door, Mrs. Mellor called, "Have you got the note for your teacher?"

"Would I forget that?" said Anne with a laugh. "Bye, Trudy! I'll see you at noon."

She was grinning as if she knew a secret. What could it be?

Trudy helped Mrs. Mellor move Anne's things back to her own room. When they came out on the front porch to begin their shopping trip, she had her first look at the street by daylight. The Mellors' two-storey house was in the middle of a row of almost identical buildings. Across the street a mix of cottages and bungalows sat on narrow lots with tiny front lawns, now sodden from the winter rains. This morning the sky was patchy with clouds. Mrs. Mellor pointed out the mountains above the opposite houses.

"That's north," she said. "You'll get a better view of the water from the corner."

Victoria Drive sloped down to the waterfront and Trudy listened politely as Mrs. Mellor pointed out Burrard Inlet and the North Shore Mountains, especially the Lions. All her life she had been used to such scenery. It was the buildings, the streetcars, the huge freighters and the crowds of people that impressed and intimidated her. Thank goodness this was just a visit!

At the next corner, Mrs. Mellor stopped. "That's Anne's school. I've sent a note to ask if you may sit in on the class one day."

So that was Anne's secret! Trudy gazed at the two-storey yellow brick building in dismay. It was so big! Did she want to go there?

"How many kids?" she asked.

"I think it's over three hundred," answered Mrs. Mellor.

"Are any Japanese?"

"Oh, yes. Japanese, Chinese, new immigrants from Europe — it's quite a mix. Are you thinking of that boy who made the tenth pupil at camp? How's he getting on?"

"He's very smart."

"They often are. Here we are on Hastings Street. This is the streetcar line we take to go downtown, but today we're going the other way to the grocery store. It's run by Chinese."

Trudy had money that Dad and Grandpa had given her.

She bought two nickel candy bars to share with Anne and Helen after school.

There was still almost an hour to put in before lunch.

"Why don't you find a book to read?" suggested Mrs. Mellor.

Helen had a full set of L.M. Montgomery's Anne books. Trudy had read *Anne of Green Gables* and *Anne of Avonlea* and was anxious to read the others. On the other hand, her friend had urged her to read *Little Men* by Louisa May Alcott. They had read *Little Women* in school last year and loved it. Then the teacher had loaned them *Good Wives*.

"I have to take this back to the library on Friday, so read it first," Anne had said the night before. "It's as good as *Little Women*."

Trudy didn't think that was possible but she opened the book now. Soon she was so wrapped up in Jo's new life that she didn't want to stop for lunch with the other girls. When they'd gone back to school, she was happy to curl up again in the easy chair in the living room. In chapter one, a boy named Nat had turned up at Jo's school. Because he was a musician, he reminded Trudy of Shigi, even though he was an orphan and played the violin, not the flute. Just like Shigi, Nat had a hard time fitting in with the other boys at school. Trudy felt very sorry for him and hoped desperately that he would finally be accepted. She was still deep in the book when Anne came home at 3:30.

"See, I was right, wasn't I?" said Anne, noting Trudy's red eyes. "It's a great story!"

Trudy smiled at her. It was good to have a friend who liked the same books you did.

"And guess what?" added Anne. "Miss Matlock says you can come to school both Friday and Monday! Well, aren't you glad?"

"I think I'm scared!" answered Trudy.

The next morning she was very nervous in a whole room full of grade six pupils.

At recess, a boy pointed at her and Anne and said, "Now there's two hicks from the sticks!"

A cold chill ran down Trudy's spine. Anne just stuck her nose in the air and said, "Get lost!"

Back in the classroom, Trudy soon found that she enjoyed doing lessons with Anne again. It was almost like old times. She liked her own small school better than this big one, but these city kids did have one thing she really envied — a library.

Every second Friday, Miss Matlock's class left school at two o'clock to march to the library in the basement of the junior high school. This time Trudy went with them. When she entered the small room, her eyes widened and she gasped in astonishment. Books filled every inch of the walls except for the door and two small, high windows. While she waited for Anne to return her books at the battered old desk in the centre of the room, she wandered along the walls reading the titles. So many books to read! How would you choose where to begin?

Anne knew exactly what she wanted. She headed for the

Alcott books and snatched at *Eight Cousins*.

"Hah! It's back! I've been waiting for this one," she said. "Now which should I take for my other one?"

"I'd like to read them all," said Trudy.

"We're only allowed two at a time," Anne said. "Mmmm, maybe I'll read *Heidi* again. I like books that make me cry."

At home that evening Anne looked up from the movie ads in Friday's paper. "Trudy, do you want to see a cowboy movie or a musical tomorrow?"

It had been arranged that on Saturday Mrs. Mellor would go downtown with the three girls to help Trudy select a length of material for summer dresses for her and Muriel. Then they'd all have lunch in Woodward's cafeteria. Afterwards, the girls would go to a movie.

"What's the musical?" asked Helen. She leaned over Anne's shoulder. "Oh! Wow! Fred Astaire and Ginger Rogers! We'll go to that."

"I asked Trudy," said her sister. "She's the guest. You can see a movie anytime. Don't pick a gangster film, Trudy. Mum would just say no. See, there's a western with Tom Mix and *Flying Down To Rio*."

"Everybody at school says Fred and Ginger are marvellous dancers," Helen said. "You'll love them, Trudy."

Trudy did like dancing. What did Anne want to see? She looked at her friend.

"I don't care which one," said Anne with a shrug. "You choose."

"Okay, I choose the musical."

Next morning, while the four of them waited in the rain for a streetcar on Hastings Street, Trudy saw a car marked Powell. She remembered that Little Tokyo where Shigi's family visited was on Powell Street. She'd like to see that.

"Could we take that streetcar?" she asked.

"We could, but we'll wait for the Hastings," answered Mrs. Mellor.

"There's no use going on Powell Street," said Helen. "The signs are all in Japanese."

"That's what makes it fun," said Anne.

"Maybe another time," their mother said before Helen could retort.

In the department store, Mrs. Mellor insisted on buying the dress material first. She and Trudy finally settled on a red background with tiny white flowers.

"Now, off you go," said Mrs. Mellor. "I'll meet you in the restaurant at a quarter to twelve. Don't go out of the store. And don't leave Trudy alone."

No, don't! thought Trudy, in alarm.

"Let's ride the escalator to the top and all the way down," said Anne.

"Oh, Anne! You're still such a child!" Helen protested. "I'm going to look at shoes. Meet me there when you've finished playing."

Secretly, Trudy found riding the escalators more fun than looking at clothes, shoes and jewelry that she couldn't buy, but she dutifully admired everything that Helen exclaimed over. Eating in the restaurant was fun. Trudy and Anne each had a hamburger with onions and relish, a mound of thick, greasy chips and a chocolate milkshake.

"Ugh!" said Helen. "You'll get pimples from that!"

"Who cares?" answered Anne. "We're not going to kiss any boys!"

Helen glared as the two of them burst into giggles.

Afterwards, they walked up the hill and joined the line-up for the matinee of *Flying Down to Rio*.

Trudy was very excited. She had seen only four movies in her whole life. One was a comedy in a church hall in Milton when she was very small. Then the one in Vancouver with Grandma. The other two were in a movie theatre in Na-naimo. She missed half of the action in one, because she fell asleep on her father's shoulder.

Today she was enthralled all the way through the film. So were Anne and Helen. They came out of the theatre so starry-eyed they never noticed the rain as they hurried back to Hastings Street, all talking at once.

"What kind of dancing did you like best? Tap? Waltz? Or the Spanish ones?"

"What colour do you think her dress was in that waltz on the ship?"

"Isn't Fred handsome?"

"How could those girls kick so high without falling over?"

"Did you see the guy who played the sax in the band? He looked like Stan Rowe, didn't he?"

Once again the Powell car passed them first. This time

Trudy never gave a thought to Shigi. Her mind was full of music and whirling dancers.

That evening, they put records on the gramophone and played Fred and Ginger. Helen always wanted to be Ginger Rogers. That was okay with the other two. They didn't mind taking turns as Fred or a member of the chorus. They found a cane that Mrs. Mellor had used once when she injured her foot. Mr. Mellor didn't own a top hat or a straw boater, so they borrowed one of his fedoras. They both became very good at twirling the cane and doffing the hat with a smile. Some of the chorus line kicks were a bit wobbly, though. Trudy became Ginger in her dreams and danced all night.

In church the next day she even had Fred and Ginger dancing in her head to the hymn tunes. Sunday School in the afternoon brought her back to earth. Anne's teacher told them about her work at an inner city mission for poor people. Men were out of work. Families were evicted for non-payment of rent. There was no money for food and clothing for the children.

"You children are privileged," she said. "You should share your good fortune with others."

Remembering the new dress material, lunch in a restaurant and the movie, Trudy put a dime instead of a nickel into the collection plate and wished it could be more.

The next day, she again went with Anne to school and that filled up Monday. Just one more day and she'd be going home, back to her own school and her rivalry with Shigi. Had he gone to school with his friends in Vancouver? What had he done on his holiday?

11

Powell Street Riot

At ten o'clock on Tuesday morning, Trudy stood at the front window and waved to Mrs. Mellor as she headed for the streetcar.

"I hate to leave you, dear," the woman had said earlier. "Tuesday is my day at the soup kitchen. We're getting more people than ever for a hot meal at noon and if I don't go, it just means the other women have to do the work and then they're late getting home. Do you mind?"

Helen and Anne took their lunch to school on Tuesdays. It was Anne's day to play basketball, which she loved. She offered to come home and have lunch with Trudy, but was relieved when Trudy told her it wasn't necessary.

"I'll be okay," she said. "I'll read."

Half an hour after opening her book, she was restless. How was she going to put in the long, lonely hours of this last day in Vancouver? It would be okay in the late afternoon. Both the girls and their mother would be home at 3:30 and Mr. Mellor was expected about the same time. What to do until then? She wished she could have gone home this morning. The family would be back in camp now. She pictured them all sitting around the table — Mum and Dad and Muriel and Karl. If she were there, they'd all be asking questions about her holiday in Vancouver. What would she tell first?

She sighed. It would be many more hours before she saw any of them. She got up and wandered to the window. The lower part of the mountains was covered in mist, but on the peaks a pale winter sun lit the snowcaps. The street was so quiet that she could hear the clang of a streetcar bell two blocks away.

It reminded her that there was one place she wanted to see in Vancouver that she hadn't yet seen, Little Tokyo. Anne said it was fun to ride down Powell on the streetcar. It wouldn't be hard. She knew where to get the streetcar at this end and if she rode as far as Woodward's store, she could just cross Hastings and come home on the next car. Maybe she would see a bit of how the Japanese people lived. If she saw Little Tokyo, she and Shigi would have something to talk about besides school work. Wouldn't it show him and his family that she was friendly?

She went upstairs and looked in the small leather change purse that Grandpa had given her for Christmas. Yes, she had enough money for carfare. Mrs. Mellor hadn't forbidden a trip to Powell Street, perhaps because she hadn't asked her. Would she be mad if Trudy went? Why? She probably wouldn't get off the streetcar, and even if she did, she was only going to walk along the street. She wouldn't go looking for the Nakano family. Still, if Vancouver kids were all in school, Shigi might be wandering around.

She came slowly back downstairs and stared at her hat and coat on the hall pegs. The house was so quiet, so empty. She couldn't stay here all day! Quickly she dressed for the outdoors. She'd be back in a couple of hours. Mrs. Mellor wouldn't even know she'd been out.

It was 11:30 when Trudy stepped off the Powell car at the east end of the street. She was alone and a little nervous. Six blocks away, at the other end of the street, a gang of about a dozen men rounded the corner from the waterfront. They were half-drunk and angry. A bend in the road hid them from Trudy.

The street was lined on both sides with stores. Many of them had display stands on the sidewalk in front of glass windows. She walked along, trying to figure out where people lived. Most of the stores had curtained windows on the second storey of the brick buildings. Perhaps that was their home. Narrow alleyways led to back premises, but she was too timid to explore them.

Her attention was caught by a woman leading a little girl by the hand. For a moment, she thought it was Mrs. Nakano and Yumi. It wasn't. She watched the woman pick up some vegetables and go inside the store to pay for them. Two older Japanese women with baskets on their arms paused at the stand, poked at a funny looking root, murmured to one another in Japanese and then moved on to the fish store next door. Trudy smiled at the carp kite hanging from the roof. That was a store sign that anyone could understand. Helen was right, though. Most of the writing was in Japanese and everyone on the street was speaking that language. When she passed people they stopped talking and stared at her. She felt uncomfortable. Then she came to a window displaying Japanese dolls in beautiful costumes. She gasped in delight. Her eyes roamed from doll to doll, taking in all the details. She was completely absorbed in them.

Suddenly, a man ran out of the store, shoved her aside and yanked down a wooden shutter over the window.

"Go, go!" he shouted. When she didn't move, he yelled something in Japanese, backed into the store and slammed the door. Trudy heard the click of the lock even over the other sounds of shutters clanging, footsteps running, mothers frantically calling children, doors and windows slamming shut. Within a minute, the street around her was deserted. What was wrong?

Different sounds now: breaking glass, angry shouts, heavy thumping. She shrank behind the brick pillar at the corner of the shop and peered fearfully toward the noise. Around a bend in the street came a mob of men, some brandishing clubs, some hurling rocks, all shouting.

"Dirty Japs!"

"Job stealers!"

"Go back where you came from!"

They were making their way down the street smashing windows and beating on door frames. Where could she hide? Everything was shut up. The street looked like a fortress and she was on the outside. Earlier she'd passed an alley. Where? She sidled back past the fish store, keeping her shoulder pressed to the wooden shutter, and there it was.

She backed in, turned around and ran a few steps. The alleyway was very narrow. Solid brick walls made it seem like a canyon. At what looked like the end, the alley bent into an even narrower and darker passage. Where did it go? Nowhere! She came up against another brick wall. This one was fitted with a lattice like the one Grandma used for climbing roses. It was much too dark in here for flowers. Panting with fright, she turned to look back the way she'd come. Judging by the noise, the mob must now be at the mouth of the alley.

"What's in here?" asked a drunken voice. The words echoed off the canyon wall.

She shrank against the lattice and a hidden door gave way, making her stumble backwards into a small room. Quickly she slammed the door shut.

When her eyes adjusted to the dark, she saw benches on two sides of the room and a wooden water bucket with a lid. A feeble light came in through a slatted, wooden roof. When she turned again to the door, she saw that it, too, had fingers of light. She put her eye to one and looked into the alley. These slits must be hidden by the bamboo lattice outside. She was in a secret room.

She sat down on a bench and breathed heavily for a few minutes. Would anyone else come here? How long would she have to stay? Could she get out? Where was the door?

In a panic, she jumped up and stood in front of the wall through which she'd entered. It looked exactly like the wall outside — brick covered with a bamboo lattice. She now realized that the bricks behind the slats were very thin. This must be the door. Where was the latch? Outside, she had just leaned on the wall and the door opened. She pushed at this side. Nothing moved. She beat on the wall with her fists. Still no movement. Her arms and legs were trembling. Think! Think! Her arms had been behind her when she leaned on the wall outside. She must have touched a latch. She put her hands in the same position just below her waist and noted the distance from the floor. Then she poked her fingers at both sides of each bamboo strip at that level. In a minute, they touched a metal bolt. She lifted it and pulled. The door opened a crack. She let out a sob of relief.

While she had been hunting for the way out, she hardly heard the frightening noises from the street, but now she

realized they were different. It sounded like men fighting.
Shouts and blows. Groans and bodies crashing into walls.
She pushed the door closed and dropped onto a bench.
There she huddled with her back against the wall and her
arms wrapped tightly around her drawn-up legs. It was as
if she were trying to make herself so small she wouldn't be
noticed if anyone came in. Tears trickled down her cheeks.
She sniffed. What a mess she'd got herself into! How was
she going to get back to the Mellor house? What would
Mrs. Mellor say when she did? Why couldn't she have gone
home today? Why did she ever come to Vancouver?

An extra loud shout made her head jerk up. Wide-eyed,
she stared at the door. What was going on out there? The
voices faded away. Now she heard another sound. Footsteps. Something scraping against the brick wall. Someone
was coming along the alley! She scrambled into the far
corner and pressed against the wall. Maybe they wouldn't
know how to get in. Don't make a sound! Don't move a
muscle! She clasped her hands tightly over her mouth to
block the scream rising in her throat.

The bars of light were blocked out. Someone was breathing in great gasps. The latch clicked. The door opened. Two
men stumbled in, a white man supporting a Japanese.

"Stan!" gasped Trudy.

Stan Rowe swore as he pushed the door shut with his
shoulder.

"Trudy! What the blazes are you doing here? Never

mind. Tell me later. I've got to tend to Tommy right now."

He eased his burden down on the bench. Trudy now recognized the other man. It was Tommy Moriyama from the blacksmith shop at home. Blood was soaking through Stan's fingers which were pressed to the back of Tommy's head.

"Is there water in that bucket, Trudy?" asked Stan.

She darted to the pail, picked up the ladle and lifted the wooden lid.

"Yes."

"Clean?"

She was a little doubtful because it was so dark in the room. "I think so."

"I've got to wash this wound and see how bad it is. Need something for a washcloth." He looked around the bare room and then down at his clothes.

"I've got a hankie in my pocket," said Trudy.

"Good! Dip it in the water and hand it over."

A million questions whirled in Trudy's brain. Why was Stan here? He couldn't have been one of the men in that ugly mob, could he? Who had hurt Tommy?

She said nothing as Stan washed the cut. Tommy winced and groaned.

"Won't be long," said Stan. "Well, it's quite deep. It's not going to stop bleeding on its own. I need a pad and a bandage to hold it in place. Here, Tommy, hold the hankie on it. I'll tear a strip off my shirt ."

He pulled the tail of his heavy plaid shirt out of his pants and tried to tear it. The flannel was too tough.

"Just a minute," said Trudy. She turned her back on the two men, reached up under her coat and dress and pulled off her half slip.

"Here," she said, holding it out to Stan.

"Thanks!"

He quickly ripped it into four pieces.

More trouble for Trudy. Mum had made that slip just two weeks ago to go with her new dress.

Stan folded one piece of cotton into a pad.

"Come and help me, Trudy," he said.

She shrank back. "I can't."

"Come on," he repeated impatiently. "Tommy's not going to bite you!"

She pressed the pad in place while Stan wound the other strips around the man's head.

She held her breath against the smell of sweat, blood, wet hair and something else. Fear? She had smelled that on herself while she crouched on the bench.

When Stan was finished, Tommy looked up and nodded, unsmiling, at each of them.

"Thanks," he said. Then he blurted out, "Why did you stop me? It just gave that guy with the rock a chance to bean me."

Stan finished drying his hands on his shirt tail.

"You were going to kill somebody," he said.

"He deserved it!" declared Tommy.

"No." Stan sat down beside Tommy and sighed. "Those guys are drunk and stupid. Somebody whipped up their hatred for the mess we're all in and told them the Orientals were to blame."

"We're only trying to make a living, like everyone else!" said Tommy.

"I know," Stan answered with another sigh. "They're aiming at the wrong target. It's the banks and the government and the other big shots they should be fighting."

"Why were you with them then?" asked the Japanese man.

It was a question Trudy wanted to ask, but she didn't like Tommy's belligerent tone.

"I dropped into the beer parlour and heard that something was up. Fool that I am, I thought maybe I could stop it," answered Stan.

A siren sounded in the distance and came closer and closer till its shriek filled the little room. It stopped abruptly and they heard the sound of tramping feet.

"The police," said Stan in a flat voice.

Tommy got up.

"Sit down," said Stan. "You can't help anyone now." Tommy hesitated. "If the police see that bandage they'll know you were involved." Tommy sat down.

The three of them listened intently. No one spoke. After about ten minutes, they heard cars starting up and driving away.

"Off to jail," said Stan. "The fools. Oh, well, at least they'll have a place to sleep and food for a few days."

"White police won't charge white men for beating up Japanese," said Tommy bitterly.

"The police will throw any unemployed man into jail, given half a chance," answered Stan, just as bitterly. "They think we're all scum."

"We?" said Tommy. "You've got a job."

"I have now."

"Can we go yet?" asked Trudy, wanting to escape the hatred in the air.

It was Tommy who answered. "Better wait," he said in a gentler voice. "Some police will be hanging around looking for stragglers." He looked at her searchingly. "Why are you here anyway?" he asked.

"Yeah!" said Stan. "I've been wondering about that."

Trudy told them.

Stan looked troubled. "Do you think you could keep quiet about all this, if I get you back before they all come home? Mellor might fire Tommy if he knew. And maybe the others, too."

He meant the other Japanese, including Mr. Nakano. Trudy nodded. She didn't intend to confess that she'd gone off on her own if she could avoid it. And she certainly didn't want to cause any trouble for Shigi and little Yumi.

Stan sighed again. "One of those goons was the kid brother of my best friend. Orrie played trumpet in our jazz band. We both lost our day jobs and then the music business dried up, too."

He got up and paced back and forth along the back wall. Tommy stood at the door, listening both to the sounds outside and to Stan. Trudy sat shivering on a bench, her eyes cast down. She knew from the rasp in Stan's voice that he was going to tell a painful story. Maybe she would, at last, have an answer to the question that had puzzled people in camp for so long. Why was such a good musician working as a logger?

Stan went on. "I talked Orrie into going to Chicago to see if we could get in a band there. It's a great jazz town. Of course we had no money for train fare. We decided . . . I persuaded him . . . to ride the rods." He stopped pacing, groaned and ran his hand over his face. "We were going to go to Winnipeg on the CPR and then head south. We got as far as Regina." He paced more quickly this time. "We had had almost no sleep and almost nothing to eat for days. We'd heard that the railway police were extra vigilant in Regina, so we waited till the train was moving pretty fast before we tried jumping on." He stopped and covered his eyes. "Orrie didn't make it. He fell under the wheels."

"Was he killed?" asked Trudy in a small voice.

Stan looked at her in a daze. He shook his head.

"No. He lost his leg. He's in a charity hospital somewhere. Sorry, Trudy. I shouldn't have told that story. I forgot you were here. You see," he added, turning to Tommy, "that's why I had to come and take care of Orrie's brother." He stood up straight and spoke briskly. "I'd better get Trudy home and go and find out what happened to him."

Tommy showed them that the back wall also contained a secret door that would let them out on Cordova Street, just a block below Hastings. As they waited for the streetcar, Trudy saw a clock on a tower down the street. It was only 2:15! It seemed as if hours had passed.

Stan walked with her as far as the block below the school.

"Don't want any of the Mellors to see me with you," he said. "They'd ask questions."

Trudy had time to go to the bathroom, wash her face and eat the sandwich Mrs. Mellor had made before anyone came home.

Just as Anne ran up the back steps, a taxi stopped at the front gate and Mr. Mellor got out.

In the excitement of greeting him and hearing about his trip, no one asked Trudy about her day. Later, Bob and Dave arrived and created more chaos. Her secret was safe.

12

Windstorm Hero

On the trip home, the three Mellors ignored Trudy except to buy her lunch on the boat. They had a lot to discuss. Mr. Mellor had received several orders for logs and his sons had seen some trucks they really liked. All three were excited about prospects for the business. Although Trudy could not forget how scared she had been in Little Tokyo, she had time to get over the worst of her fright by the time Mr. Mellor dropped her off at home.

There she found Muriel and Karl dancing with excitement in the doorway. Karl began talking as she walked up the steps.

"You should have come home yesterday," he said. "There were two dead cougars and we saw them!"

"They were monsters!" Muriel said. "Six feet long!"

"No, they weren't!" her brother said scornfully.

"They were big!" insisted Muriel.

Between them, they told the story. Some of the men from the bunkhouse had found three dead deer in the woods. They knew that if the cougars killed too many deer there wouldn't be enough animals for them to shoot for meat next fall. So two men and their dogs set off on a cougar hunt and came back with two carcasses.

"One got away," said Muriel.

"They should have taken Shaggy," said Karl. "He'd have found the other one."

"I wish they hadn't wounded the animal," said Mum. "A wounded cougar is likely to hang around camp looking for easy pickings. You'll have to keep a sharp eye on Shaggy."

Mary also had a story to tell. A cousin of the Johnson family had drowned in a boating accident along with two other young men. One of them was Japanese. Mary had been to the funeral, the first she'd ever attended. She had to tell Trudy all about it. It was easy for Trudy to keep her promise to Stan. When she had told about the movie and Woodward's and Anne's big school, everyone was satisfied.

School began on Monday and little Bertie Dodd came. Since they didn't need him to make up the numbers, Mrs. Dodd had thought she'd keep him at home until September. Bertie had other ideas. He had been promised that he could go to school after Christmas and he intended to go. Yumi Nakano, who was old enough to start, didn't come.

At recess the first day Trudy asked Shigi about that.

He shrugged. "Mother wants her at home," he said and turned back to his notebook.

He was like that for several weeks. He was polite in class and worked with the other kids when necessary but at recess he stayed inside and studied.

Trudy understood why he acted as he did. The concert and the trouble in Vancouver must have frightened and disgusted him. In January, when the radio news was full of the Powell Street Riot, the kids at school had talked about it.

Nick Carley spoke out loud enough for Shigi to hear. "My Dad says those guys shouldn't have got thrown in the clink. They should have got medals."

Trudy saw Shigi's neck muscles tighten. Was there going to be a fight? The fear she had felt in that little room on Powell Street swept over her again.

"Shut up, Nick," she said. "The Japanese are only trying to make a living, like everybody else."

"Oh, yeah!" answered Nick. "Well, if they all went back where they came from, white men could have their jobs."

Trudy retorted, "If everybody in this camp went back to the country they came from, there wouldn't be many people left!"

No wonder Mrs. Nakano wouldn't let Yumi come to school. No wonder Shigi ignored everyone.

Shigi concentrated on his school work. He no longer brought the flute to accompany the anthem, although he still played duets with his mother. Stan still called at the Nakano house about once a week for an evening of music. On these winter nights, the path along Black Creek was very dark. Shigi would meet Stan at the railway bridge with a lantern and go back that far with him afterwards.

At parting, Stan always said, "Don't let the cougars get you!"

It was a joke. If Stan really thought there was a cougar around, he wouldn't have let Shigi come out. Anyway, a cougar wouldn't attack a moving person carrying a light. It liked to pounce on prey that was still and quiet.

A more definite danger was the old railway bridge. Mr. Mellor had a crew working all out to get the new truck bridge finished. He didn't seem to care that the train crossing needed some repairs. People on foot had to be careful to avoid broken boards.

One day in March, Bertie Dodd asked to be excused to use the outhouse. When he opened the school door, they all heard a high whining sound.

"What's that?" asked the little boy.

Miss Lewis came to stand beside him. "A wind storm coming, I think."

"I'm scared," said Bertie.

"Al, you go with Bertie," Miss Lewis said. "And hurry back."

By the time they returned, the wind was roaring. A few drops of rain hit the windows.

"I think you'd better all go home," said the teacher. "If we wait till four o'clock, you'll get soaked."

She stood on the porch and watched the children push against the wind. The older ones were holding on tight to the youngsters. Across the river, the trees by the stream were bending and shaking. Shigi came out last.

"It might be dangerous on the path by Black Creek," she said. "Do you want to come to my house until the storm is over?"

"No, thank you," Shigi answered. "My mother and sister are alone. They will be frightened. I must go home."

The teacher held up her hand. "Listen!" In a lull in the storm they heard the work whistle. "Isn't that the quitting whistle? Your father will go home."

"They are working far up the hill. It will take him much longer than me. I must go."

"Very well. Go quickly and be careful."

In the logged-off area of the camp there were no trees to blow down, but Shigi saw the men in the blacksmith shop lashing the tin roof with ropes to hold it in place. He struggled against the wind, sometimes walking backwards to catch his breath. When he reached the mill, he rested for a few minutes. The men paid no attention to him as they were too busy securing anything that might blow away. The storm was certainly fierce. It reminded him of their old home at Storm Inlet. Although he had never experienced a wind like this on shore, he had often looked out at the ocean and seen fishing boats tossing about on huge waves. When his father was out in the boat, his mother was terrified. She would be just as frightened now.

He took a deep breath and stepped out into the rain once more. The wet ties of the railway bridge were slippery. Because of the rain, he could hardly see where to place his feet. The bridge swayed and creaked in the wind. He was glad to step off on the other side of the river. His father and his friends had built the footbridge across Black Creek and he felt safer on it, but the path through the woods held another danger. Branches fell all around him. Looking up, he saw that the trees were leaning far over. If one fell, it could crush him to death. He walked as fast as he dared over the debris on the path and then ran the last few steps and tumbled into the house.

His mother grabbed him in a fierce hug. Yumi, who was crouching under the low table, whimpered as something hit the roof with a thud. Shigi stared upward. The ceiling looked flimsy when he thought of the looming trees near the path. Perhaps they would be safer in the bathhouse which was partially protected by the house.

His mother agreed. "Quickly, roll up the quilts. Take some blankets." The trembling in her arms and hands stopped now that she had something to do. "Yumi, put on your raincoat. Hurry! Hurry!"

The bathhouse was small and sturdy. The Japanese men had built two of them: one for the three men and one for the Nakano family. It was Shigi's job at the end of each work day to haul water up from the creek and fill the baths. Then he lit the fires that would heat the water by the time the men came off shift.

Mrs. Nakano spread quilts on the floor. She wrapped Yumi in a blanket and sat down close beside her. Shigi knew he couldn't light the fire because the strong wind would blow the sparks. He took down the kerosene lantern from its bracket on the wall, lit it and placed it on the bench near his mother's shoulder. Although it gave very little heat, the light was cheerful.

After a while, Shigi thought the gusts of wind were coming less often and were not as strong. In one lull, he could even hear the roar of the creek and the rain beating on the roof. There came one last, terrifying blast and then the wind stopped for a few seconds, as if catching its breath.

Into the relative silence came an even more terrifying sound. Seven toots on the woods whistle! The signal for an accident.

As the wind started up again, the Nakanos stared at one another, wide-eyed with fright.

≈

At the bunkhouse, the cook heard the misery whistle. Stan Rowe was at work in the woods, so it was the cook's job to pack the supplies and stretchers for the rescue crew. When the packs were ready, two men ran into the first aid room, picked them up and dashed through the rain to the speeder where Fred was waiting to rush them to the scene of the accident.

The Nakano family heard them pass on the other side of the creek. Like all the other families in camp, they could do nothing except wait.

Shigi listened to the water racing toward the river. He pictured it roiling and boiling against the pilings of the old bridge. Were they strong enough to withstand the flood? He thought of how the timbers had creaked and groaned when he crossed earlier that afternoon. They had obviously held while the speeder crossed. What would happen when it came back? He paced restlessly around and around the bath. Suddenly he turned to his mother.

"I'm going to check the bridge pilings," he said.

She didn't want him to go and wouldn't agree until he reminded her that it might be his father who was being taken across the river in the speeder.

"It's pitch black out there," she said. "Take the lantern."

Dressed in his high rubber boots, black slicker and fisherman's rain hat, he stepped out toward the stream. If he was going to inspect the pilings, he'd have to be at water level. That meant hiking along the creek to the river and then along its bank to the bridge. It was dangerous. The rocks and mud on the bank were slippery. The lantern shed only a small pool of light at his feet so he couldn't see what was ahead, although the splash of the water against fallen branches gave him some warning of snags. Whenever he could, he clung to bushes with his free hand. Sometimes he had to wade into the water. When he reached the river he could feel the pull of the current and knew that if he fell he'd be swept away.

Ah! There was the bridge!

Exhausted, he leaned against the nearest post for a moment. Was all this effort wasted? It was too dark for him to see the pilings beyond his lantern light and there was no way he could get close to them.

He didn't have to.

When he swung the light on to the post against which he rested, he found a long, deep crack. Shigi stared into the river and saw that the post was swaying slightly. The force of the water had loosened it. As soon as the weight of the speeder struck the bridge, that post would collapse.

He had to warn the speederman.

Clinging to bushes whose roots were exposed by the eroding soil, and slipping back one step for every two he went forward, he scrambled up to the line.

The wind had picked up again and the rain was driving straight into his face. He wouldn't be able to see the speeder coming and he might not hear it above the wind. Should he stay on the ties or try to walk beside the track? If he did that, the driver might not see him till too late. He'd stay on the ties and take his chances.

When he thought he had walked far enough from the

bridge so that Fred could stop the speeder, he stood still. He was so tired! He couldn't go another step! Both his feet were soaking wet. He remembered freezing water pouring into his right boot once when he slipped. The other probably filled up with rain water running off his slicker.

He peered down the track. Was that a light ahead? Yes! It was coming closer. He waved his lantern in a slow arc. The speeder was moving at a snail's pace behind a man carrying a lantern like his. It stopped.

He told about the bridge.

After hearing the boy's report, the rescue crew decided to get the crummy and take the injured men to camp on the old road.

When one man set off to fetch the truck, Fred turned to Shigi.

"Thanks, kid. You probably saved some lives. Those injured guys wouldn't have been able to swim if we'd gone into the river." He peered at the boy more closely. "You're soaked. Get home now, out of this storm."

Shigi hadn't moved from the spot he'd been standing on when the speeder stopped. He took a step forward.

"Who's hurt?" he croaked.

Fred answered quickly. "Not your Dad. Not any of the Japs."

Shigi's shoulders slumped in relief.

"There's three of them," the other man said. "A tree fell on Pete and Andy. Stan was trying to help them when a branch came down."

A cold hand seemed to grip Shigi's neck. "Stan Rowe?" he whispered.

"Yeah. But he's not too bad. Just his hand crushed. He'll probably lose that, but he's luckier than the other two."

Shigi turned away and stumbled toward home. Stan lucky to lose only a hand? He'd never play the sax again.

13

Cougar

On the night that the three injured men were taken out to the hospital, Trudy had a terrifying nightmare. Her mother heard her sobs. Trudy first sensed her presence in the doorway and then felt a comforting pat on her legs. Because she slept against the wall, that was the only part that Mum could reach.

"Ssh! Ssh! Don't wake the other kids," whispered Mum. "Crawl over the end of the bed. There's probably still a bit of heat in the stove. We'll sit in the other room."

Soon they were cuddled up together under a blanket on the chesterfield.

"What's wrong, Trudy? Are you worried about Stan?" asked Mum.

"Yes," said Trudy. She blinked back more tears. "Why did he have to get hurt? He's one of the good guys. He tried to stop the fight."

"What are you talking about?"

Trudy gulped and then told the whole story of the riot on Powell Street.

"I'm sorry about ripping up my slip, Mum," she said at the end.

Her mother hugged her tightly.

"Oh, Trudy, you do fuss about all the wrong things! Who cares about a lost slip when you might have been badly hurt?"

Trudy sighed. She was glad that she had finally confessed.

"Stan said not to tell," she added. "You won't, will you?"

"No. No," promised her mother. "I'm glad you told me. It's best to talk scary things out."

"Why did it happen, Mum? Why were those men so mean?"

"Oh, Trudy, it's such a big question!"

"But I need to know!"

Mum sighed. "Well, for one thing, there are so many men out of work right now. It upsets them that they can't take care of their families. They get mad so they pick on people that they think are better off than they are."

"Mr. Carley has a job. Why does he pick on the Japanese?"

"Probably because they're different. It was the same

when my parents first came to Canada from Norway," answered Mum.

Trudy jerked upright and stared at her mother. "Grandpa and Grandma Holm? But everyone thinks Grandpa's great. And everyone loves Grandma."

"They do now. But they had a very hard time when they first came here. People couldn't understand Grandpa's English. They thought he and Grandma dressed funny and ate queer food. Even when I went to school, the other kids used to make fun of my smelly fish lunches." She laughed. "Sometimes I used to bury the sandwiches beside the path."

"Then you'd go hungry!" said Trudy.

"Oh, one of the other girls used to share her lunch with me. She didn't mind being teased for befriending me."

"I like that girl!" said Trudy.

"So did I," answered Mum with a laugh. Then she spoke very soberly. "I'm afraid, Trudy, that it's human nature to fear and distrust people who are different. It takes a real effort to see beyond the differences to what a person is really like. My friend made that effort and you're making it with Shigi. I'm proud of you." She hugged Trudy again and then threw off the blanket. "Now, kid, go back to bed and sleep or you won't want to get up in the morning."

Tucked in beside Muriel again, Trudy had a lot to puzzle about. She fell asleep before she found any answers.

On Sunday, Tom Paine went to the hospital in Nanaimo

with Mr. Mellor to visit the patients. The other two men were still there, but Stan had left. The nurse said that since he had an appointment with the doctor on Tuesday, he was probably still in town. Tom found him in a boarding house. He was lying on his back staring up at the ceiling. His injured hand, in a big bandage, rested on the very edge of the bed. It was as if he were trying to push it away and forget it.

Back home, Tom reported to the family.

"The doctor amputated Stan's thumb and first finger. They think they can save the rest."

"Will he be able to play the sax?" asked Trudy.

Her Dad shrugged. "Who knows? Right now, he thinks he'll never play again, but who knows? Lots of injured men learn to cope."

Trudy thought of Stan's friend Orrie. Had he learned to walk again with only one leg?

"Is he coming back, Dad?" asked Karl.

"No. He can't work with that hand. He asked me to pack up his gear."

"Where will he go?" Mum asked in a worried voice.

"To his family in Vancouver. That's where he said to send his stuff."

Just before bedtime, Dad came back from the bunkhouse. Karl was already in his pyjamas as the three kids sat at the table having a cup of cocoa.

"Stan wanted you kids each to have something." He

pulled a softball and a harmonica box out of his jacket pocket. "For Muriel and Karl. Which do you want?"

"The ball!" said Karl. "I've got a mouth organ."

He tossed the ball from hand to hand.

"That okay with you, Muriel?" asked her Dad.

Muriel nodded. A tear fell into the box as she lifted out the shiny instrument. Trudy knew how she felt. Why couldn't they have Stan back, instead of something to remember him by?

What was her present? Dad pulled a piece of white paper from inside his jacket and laid it face up in front of her.

It was a 5 by 7 glossy photo of Stan. Full length. With his saxophone held high, ready to play. A much younger Stan. Stan with a big grin on his face, ready to conquer the world of jazz.

"That's his publicity photo," exclaimed Mum. "Won't he need it?"

"He said to give it to Trudy," Dad answered firmly.

"Let me see," said Karl, reaching across the table.

Trudy put her thumbs down on the corners of the photo, anchoring it. Muriel and Karl came around and leaned on either side of her. Mum and Dad looked over her shoulder.

For a moment they all gazed at their friend in silence.

Then Muriel said, "Lucky you!"

"I know," answered Trudy quietly.

Mum leaned down and put her cheek on Trudy's hair. "Somewhere I've got one of those cardboard frames you get from a photographer. I'll find it tomorrow."

"Thanks," said Trudy, not trusting her voice to say any more.

Trudy told Shigi about Stan on Monday morning. It was easier to talk to the Japanese boy now because for a few days he was a hero. When Mr. Mellor examined the bridge he knew that stopping the speeder had saved the lives of the injured men.

The boss decided not to repair the bridge. It was braced temporarily so that the speeder could cross, but the old Shay engine was left to rust in the woods. The whole camp was excited about the next phase of the operation — logging with trucks.

Ten days after the storm, on a Tuesday afternoon, an air of expectancy hung over the camp. From noon on, somebody was always peering down the road to the lake. Dave and Bob Mellor had gone to Nanaimo the day before to pick up the new truck. Everyone hoped to be the first to see it. The school outhouse was in constant use all afternoon and everyone who went out took a long time both coming and going. Women came across the bridge on any excuse. Mr. Mellor kept stepping out of his office and looking down the road. Whenever he wasn't out there, the cook or his helpers or the blacksmiths or the men from the mill were.

Just as school was dismissed at four o'clock, the kids heard horns honking. In less than a minute the road was lined with people on both sides. Mr. Mellor stood in the middle of the road, hands on hips, staring at the bend around which the truck would come.

And there it was! Trudy gasped. It was huge! It towered over the car which was leading it into camp. Its red paint was ten times shinier than the rusted green Chev. The honk of its horn was ten times as loud. Only the grins on the faces of the two Mellor boys were the same. They matched their father's smile as he motioned them to stop.

Everyone pressed forward and examined some part of the truck from the shiny grill to the huge tires. Mr. Mellor climbed up into the cab with Bob and leaned out of the open door.

"We're going to take her across the new bridge," he said. "Where's that kid who stopped the speeder? Shigi? Come on up here, boy. You can ride in the cab. Anyone else can climb on the back there."

With Dave's help, all the kids scrambled up on to the flat bed where the logs would ride. Trudy looked down at her mother and laughed. It was fun to be riding so high above her. When she glanced through the window at the back of the cab, Shigi's excitement and pride showed in the set of his shoulders. It was only fair that he had the honour of riding up front.

Everyone except Nick and Al crowded into the centre of the truck when it crossed the bridge. Trudy grabbed Karl and Eddie while Mary hung on to Bertie and Lorraine. It was a long, long way down to the water! On the other side, Bob stopped at the old road. Everyone jumped down.

"Now, listen, kids," said the boss. "You've all had a ride on this new truck. From now on it's hands off. Get it? I don't want to see any of you anywhere near this baby. Understood?"

Everyone nodded, although Nick and Al looked sulky. Trudy knew they were jealous of Shigi's ride in the cab.

Spring came early to the Cowichan Valley. There were several warm, sunny days in May. One weekend, Ellie Paige decided to begin her spring cleaning. That meant plenty of work for the whole family for about a week. The first thing to do was take down the stovepipes, clean out the soot and put them back. Tom would do that on Sunday morning. That meant the three kids had to stay out of the house. Tom hated the job and didn't want anyone around while he did it. Ellie knew that he would end up swearing and she didn't want the children to hear.

Muriel and Karl went off on a picnic with the Dodds. Trudy was invited, but she wanted to read her new book, *What Katy Did* by Susan Coolidge. It had come from Anne Mellor in Wednesday's mail. In her note Anne said she had cried buckets. When Trudy opened the parcel on Wednesday, she looked at the pictures, read the first page and shivered with excitement. She decided to leave the book till she could settle down for a good, long read.

Now was her chance. She made sandwiches for Muriel and Karl to take on the picnic and one for herself. When they'd left, she headed off with Shaggy towards the railroad bridge. Across the tracks Trudy had a hidey-hole overlooking the river where an osier bush grew around a boulder that made a backrest. Already the pale green leaves on the red branches gave enough shelter to screen her from anyone coming along the path. Not that anyone would on a Sunday. Only Black Creek, where the Japanese lived, was past this spot and no one ever went there. In fact, Tommy's old truck was not parked in the usual place, so maybe they were away.

With a sigh of contentment, she opened her book. Shaggy made a tour of the bush, sniffed at a rock on the right and then settled down beside her and went to sleep. For an hour, the dog and the girl were off in another world.

Then Shaggy stirred, opened his eyes and lifted his nose. He rose quickly and growled low in his throat. Trudy looked up from her book. In his youth, Shaggy had been a good hunting dog. Even though Trudy had never been hunting with him, she recognized his stance.

"What is it, Shaggy?" she asked from her seat on the ground. "Raccoons?"

Not raccoons. The dog would bark and chase them. A deer, maybe? She got up quietly and stood behind him and peered into the bush along the creek. Nothing.

Still growling very low, Shaggy walked forward almost soundlessly. Excited now, Trudy followed him as silently as she could. Although some sunlight filtered through the trees, there were pockets of deep shadow. Deer could hide in these by keeping perfectly still. Trudy stared and stared, moving her head slowly in a big semicircle. Nothing. She glanced down at the dog, He was looking not at the ground but up into a tree beside the path. She followed his gaze and gasped aloud. A cougar!

The long, tawny body lay along a branch of a young Douglas fir. The animal was not looking at her and Shaggy. Could this be the one the men had wounded in the eye back in January? Maybe it couldn't see them. It was concentrating on something, though. What? She looked to the left and went rigid with fright.

Little Yumi Nakano was crouched on the edge of the path, half hidden by a bush. She was staring up at the cougar. She seemed mesmerized by the cat's stillness.

14

Shigi's Home

As Trudy looked from the cat to the little girl, all the advice she'd ever heard about what to do if she saw a cougar raced through her mind.

Stand up and keep moving. A cougar won't attack a human being unless it's really desperate. Yumi was cringing like a frightened rabbit.

Yell. When the cougar hears answering voices, it will take off. Who would hear her away out here in the woods? Her voice would never reach the camp. Maybe Shaggy's bark would. The other dogs would surely hear it. Shaggy was so old and slow. Would he have a chance against the cat? Would the noise startle the cougar into leaping at the little girl?

Go for help. The cougar would attack long before she

found anyone. Although it seemed minutes that she stood petrified, it was really only seconds. What she had to do was to divert the cat's attention from the child.

"Bark, Shaggy!" she ordered.

"Help! Help!" she yelled.

The sleek head swung toward them.

"Go home, Yumi!" yelled Trudy.

The little girl didn't move.

When Shaggy obeyed the order to bark, his voice came out as a baying sound that Trudy had never heard. Was it a hunting signal? Would the other camp dogs recognize it? Even if the hunters followed the dogs, would they be there in time?

Yumi must get away.

"Yumi, go home! The cougar's not watching you. Go!"

The child stayed still.

Someone was crashing through the bush behind Trudy. She took a swift glance backwards. Shigi! With a rod and a string of fish.

"What? What?" he asked frantically.

"It's a cougar," she answered quickly. "And Yumi."

He dropped the rod and the fish. Trudy could almost hear the thoughts racing through his head. Shaggy was still baying and Trudy yelled to keep the cougar's attention on them.

"Take her home," Shigi said.

He picked up the string of fish and threw them in the opposite direction to Yumi. The cougar looked toward the sound. Trudy quickly edged to the side of the little girl. Yumi was standing now, but she didn't move. Trudy took her arm to pull her along. It was like dragging a rock. Should she try to carry her?

Shigi called something in Japanese.

The child awoke as if from a daze. She whimpered.

"Go with Trudy, Yumi! Go home! Don't run," he added in a frantic tone.

As if Trudy didn't know that! She took Yumi's hand and walked briskly along the path. Behind her she heard the welcome sounds of dogs barking and men yelling. Then ahead of them appeared Mrs. Nakano, running and calling her daughter's name.

She snatched the child up in one arm, reached the other hand out to Trudy and ran back home.

The first few minutes inside were spent in sobbing, scolding and explaining. Yumi said she thought it would be fun to hide in the bushes and surprise Shigi on his way home from fishing. When Mrs. Nakano heard the barking and yelling, she went out to look for her daughter in the garden where she should have been playing with her dolls. Trudy told how she and Shaggy happened to be there when the cougar appeared.

"You saved Yumi," said the mother, giving her child another hug.

A minute later, Shigi ran in. He went straight to his sister, took her hand and held it against his cheek while murmuring in Japanese. Mrs. Nakano sank on to a floor cushion with Yumi still in her arms. Everything had to be explained all over again for Shigi.

Then the boy said to Trudy, "Your father says you are to stay here until he comes for you. Two men with guns are hunting the cougar. Your father has gone to warn the Dodd family. When it is safe, he will come here."

Mrs. Nakano set Yumi down and got up from the floor. Although she was still trembling, she bowed formally.

"Excuse us for not greeting you properly," she said. "Welcome to our house, Shigi's schoolmate."

Shigi and Yumi also bowed. Feeling a little silly, Trudy bowed back.

She looked around. The house was just one big room with open rafters for a ceiling. One corner was obviously the kitchen. In another corner, rolled bedding was stacked against folded screens. Large floor cushions made seats under one window. Near the window there was a niche in the wall, lined with photographs of Japanese people. A scroll of paper with printing on it hung in front. On a small table were a vase of flowers, a small sculpture of Buddha and a burning candle. Trudy's attention had been caught by the printing on the scroll. Was it rude to stare?

"That is our shrine to our ancestors," Shigi explained.

"Why do you have Skuli Johnson's name on that paper?" Trudy asked.

Mrs. Nakano bowed to the shrine before answering in a gentle voice.

"There was a boating accident. My sister's son was

drowned with two other young men. We honour them all."
She pointed to each name. "Skuli Johnson, Joe Richards
and this in Japanese characters is Shigi's cousin, also Shigi."

Trudy looked at her classmate. All the times that Mary
talked about her cousin and received everybody's sympa-
thy, Shigi had never once said that his cousin died in the
same accident. And yet his family remembered all three
young men. She felt ashamed.

Yumi broke the mood by asking Trudy if she would like
to see her dolls.

"No. You left them outside," said her mother. "It's not
safe to go out."

"I'll bring them in," said Shigi.

In a minute he returned with a red lacquered chest.

"It's quiet out there," he reported. "They must have
chased the cougar up into the hills."

The dolls were as beautiful as the ones Trudy had seen in
the window on Powell Street. She exclaimed over the
colourful kimonos and the elegant hair styles.

"Where did you get them all?" asked Trudy.

"This one is from my grandmother and this is from my
aunt." Yumi cradled the smallest of the dolls in her hand.
"My other grandmother send me this. It's very old. Her
mother gave it to her."

"All Japanese girls have a doll collection," said Mrs.
Nakano. She smiled. "I still have mine. Would you like to
see it?"

"Not now," said Shigi. "I want to show her my water carrier."

Reluctantly, Mrs. Nakano agreed that they could go down to the stream. On the way they stopped at the bathhouse and Shigi explained how he filled the two baths every day and heated the water.

"First my father and I bathe and then my mother and sister."

A bath every day! Everyone Trudy knew had a bath on Saturday night unless something special was happening. No wonder Shigi always looked so clean!

"At first I lugged every bucketful by hand. Then I got smart and built this." He pointed to a wheel with a handle and a rope looped over it. They followed the rope down to the stream and another wheel.

"I can hook two buckets on the rope and carry a third one. It sure saves time. What I'd really like is a way of dumping the buckets into the bath and bringing them back down. That needs a much bigger framework and wheel. Maybe I won't have time for that."

Trudy hardly heard the last remark. She was very impressed with what he had already done.

"How did you think this up?" she asked.

"Oh, I read a lot of stuff about machines and buildings. I'm going to be an engineer some day."

"You're sure smart!"

"So are you," answered Shigi. "You'll go to university, too."

Trudy laughed. "Me? Not likely." She looked at him shyly. "I would like to be a teacher some day."

"You'd be a good one," he said.

Just then, Mrs. Nakano called them in for lunch. Shigi had forgotten to pick up the fish he'd caught, so they had dried fish, rice and greens from the garden. Yumi showed Trudy how to squat at the low table. Amid much laughter, they all tried to teach her to use chopsticks. Everyone cheered when she finally picked up a piece of fish and put it in her mouth. Next, she nipped some greens. They had a funny, tart taste, but she politely swallowed them. The rice defeated her. With a smile, Mrs. Nakano handed her a spoon.

When Tom Paige came to collect his daughter, she was in the garden with Yumi and Mrs. Nakano. Most of the spring vegetables had not yet been planted, but there were still some winter cabbages and a row of new chard leaves like they'd had at lunch. Mrs. Nakano made a parcel of vegetables and insisted they take it.

"It is not a proper thank you," she said. "When my husband comes home, he will think of something suitable."

"No need for thanks," said Tom Paige. "You and I can both be proud of our kids. Your boy prevented a bad accident at the bridge and my Trudy seems to have behaved bravely." He smiled at Yumi. "The cougar's dead. The kids are all safe. That's what matters."

Mary, Frieda, Muriel and Karl raced to meet Trudy as

soon as she and her father crossed the tracks. They wanted to hear all about the cougar and the Japanese house. They shivered with terror when she told them about the big cat. When she described the Nakano home — the bath house, the rolled up bedding and the low table — they giggled and made silly remarks.

"Can't they afford proper beds?" asked Mary.

"They eat off the floor?" exclaimed Frieda in exaggerated surprise.

"No! They eat off the table; they sit on the floor."

Trudy stopped talking. She hated it that the kids made fun of the Nakanos. To her, the Japanese house was different, but it wasn't something to make fun of. She had seen it as a family home, like their own. Of course, her family didn't have a shrine. But they did keep special pictures on the top shelf of the sideboard. Grandma and Grandpa Holm were there. And the other grandparents. And Uncle Ted Paige, who had died in an accident. And Stan Rowe. It was a place of honour, something like a shrine.

15

Sore Losers

Feelings between the loggers and the Japanese did not improve after the May 24th picnic at the old Camp 5 on the lake. Mellor's Camp and Drew's Camp 6 met there for a day of fun and food. All the families went and many of the loggers. Mr. Mellor and Mr. Drew donated prize money for a baseball tournament — twenty dollars to the winning team, a dollar to the pitcher with the most strike-outs and a dollar to the batter who scored the most runs. Each of the Camps organized a team.

All five of the Japanese men loved baseball. They were envious when they saw the notice about the tournament. They knew they would not be invited to play on the Mellor's team. But there were three Japanese men working at Camp 6. So Tommy Moriyama persuaded his friends to enter an all-Japanese team. With Shigi, they'd have nine players.

Bill Carley objected to allowing the new team to play.

"Those Japs want to horn in on everything," he said. "Baseball's our game."

The bosses disagreed.

Mr. Drew said, "It's an open challenge. Anyone can get up a team and enter."

"The more teams, the more fun," Mr. Mellor said.

The tournament took most of the day to play. There were lots of other things to do — games for the children, swimming for those brave enough to face the cold water, eating and visiting old friends. A long tablecloth had been laid on the ground and covered with food. Nick and Al and some of the boys from Camp 6 had an eating contest. Even after that was over there was plenty left.

Mealtime as usual was a time for storytelling. Mrs. Dodd told about the day Bertie was lost. As she spoke, mothers from both camps hugged their young children close. The end of the story, when Shaggy found Bertie, reminded the Camp 6 people of the time one of their dogs was gored by a moose.

"It was early morning," one of the women began. "I was just thinking of getting up when I heard our young pup yip yapping like crazy. I put on my dressing gown and went out to shut him up before he woke the kids. At first I couldn't see him. He wasn't on our wharf or on Todd's next door. So I went around to the shore side and I saw him a few yards away barking at a huge moose that had just stepped out of the lake. I'd never seen a moose that close before. And I never want to see one again! It was a scary sight, but funny too. This little tiny dog telling this huge moose to vamoose! And the moose just standing there, dripping water and swaying its head back and forth. It seemed to be trying to figure out what this noisy thing was. Of course, it could have trampled the pup to death with one stomp of its hoof. I yelled at the pup to come home, but of course he didn't. While I tried to make up my mind what to do, two other dogs arrived on the scene."

"My Peggy," interrupted one boy proudly.

"And our Toby," chorused two girls.

"That's right," said the storyteller. "So Toby and Peggy went straight for the moose. One went to the back and nipped at its heels."

"Peggy," said the boy.

"And the other stood in front and barked at its head. They were trying to protect the pup. Anyway, the moose suddenly seemed to get tired of all the racket. It gave a great bellow, lowered its head and charged at Toby. It caught him with the tip of one of its antlers and tossed him aside. Then it strode off into the bush. By this time all sorts of people were outside in their pyjamas and Toby was well taken care of."

"Did anyone kill the moose?"

"No. It was the wrong season. No moose steaks."

"Too bad."

Mrs. Paige told the story of the cougar that nearly got little Yumi Nakano.

And the Camp 6 kids told about the day they were on the school float and the smallest of them fell into the water. Someone went in to rescue him but couldn't do it. So another jumped in and another and another until they were all in the lake, getting in one another's way so that no one could get out. The teacher came with a boat hook, caught the little one by the seat of his pants and hauled him up. The rest followed and all got sent home to change their clothes. No more school that day.

"Speaking of getting soaking wet," said Trudy. She told about the big·storm and how Shigi stopped the speeder at the bridge.

In spite of all that was going on, there were always a few spectators at the baseball field. For the last inning of the final game, almost everyone was there. The two teams were Mellor's Camp and the Japanese. Camp 6 had been defeated by Pete's brilliant pitching for Mellor's and Harold Yoshida's batting for the Japanese.

When Trudy arrived, the Japanese team had a runner on first base and Shigi was at bat. She cheered loudly when he hit a grounder to centre field. The runner on first ran to third and Shigi slid safely into second. Trudy was the only one clapping. Nick scowled at her.

"Traitor," he said.

Trudy was torn. She did want her Dad's team to win. On the other hand, she was sorry that no one was rooting for Shigi's team. But she groaned as loudly as everyone else on the next play when Mellor's short stop dropped the ball and Tommy Moriyama was safe at first.

Score tied four to four. Bases loaded. Two out. And Yoshida up to bat!

The crowd was yelling wildly. It was now a contest between two superb players, Pete and Harold. Pitcher and batter eyed each other while the onlookers shouted encouragement or insults.

Pete wound up, The crowd fell silent as the ball sped toward home plate. Harold stopped swaying and swung his bat in a graceful arc that caught the ball squarely and sent it out of the field. Another home run for Yoshida!

The Japanese won, eight to four.

Most of the men were good sports about it. They knew the Japanese had played a great game. Bill Carley gathered a few sore losers around him at the prize-giving ceremony. Pete had pitched the most strikeouts and Harold had scored the most runs.

Carley knew he couldn't stop the winning team from getting the twenty dollars.

"Okay, they won the twenty bucks," he said. "But Yoshida's getting a share of that. He shouldn't get any more."

His friends growled their assent.

Mr. Drew saw that the ugly feelings could end up in a fight, spoiling the day for everyone.

He shrugged. "Sounds fair," he said. He handed the money to Pete and to the runner-up in runs, a man from his own camp.

Back at school next day, Nick tried to pick a fight with Shigi.

"You guys were just lucky," he said.

Al and Karl wouldn't go along with him. They both admired the way Shigi handled the bat.

Trudy tried to tell Shigi that she thought Harold Yoshida had been treated unfairly.

He wouldn't talk about it. He just grinned gleefully. "We whomped them!"

Miss Lewis rang the bell to end recess before Karl could answer.

16

Test of Friendship

The trial of the men who had been arrested after the Powell Street Riot began on a hot day in June 1935. Six white men and three Japanese, who had been out on bail, now appeared in court. In the newspapers and on the radio the trial was big news. Editorials and letters to the editor inflamed the anti-Oriental feelings of many people. Extra police guarded the Vancouver Courthouse as an angry mob waited in the street each day after the spectators' gallery was filled. They shouted and jeered when the Japanese prisoners were brought out and cheered for the others.

In Mellor's Camp, Jimmy Wallace, one of the recently hired men, was extremely anti-Japanese. His brother was on trial. He was a very persuasive talker and he soon had many of the loggers on his side.

Trudy looked at the pictures in the newspaper. She heard people talking about the trial. She was amazed at how quickly the bad feeling spread. It was like the time the measles had hit Camp Six. One day all the kids had been at school healthy and happy. Within a week they were all at home, sick and miserable. Was hatred catching like the measles? How could people believe that the Japanese they knew were evil? Then she remembered Tommy Moriyama. He had been ready to kill someone. If Stan hadn't stopped him, he'd be on trial, too. She had nightmares again.

One morning at recess, Nick Carley was bursting with news. He gathered all the older kids around him behind the school.

"Know what?" he asked. "Them Japs are all spies!"

"Shut up, Nick," said Frieda. "Dad said we weren't to talk about it yet."

For a moment Nick glared at his sister. Then he slouched as though the steam had gone out of him.

"Oh, yeah! I forgot." He straightened up. "Anyway, if he knows what's good for him, that judge better not jail any of those guys who were in the fight."

"Does that include the Japanese?" asked Shigi from the edge of the group.

"Naw! He'll send them back to their own country!"

"Where's that?" asked Shigi. "They're all Canadian citizens."

As Nick lunged toward him, Shigi slipped around the corner of the building where Miss Lewis was playing dodge ball with the little kids.

For a few days, Trudy worried about what Nick had said. Then, when she was alone with Mary and Frieda at the swimming hole, she asked Frieda. They were sitting on the riverbank wrapped in towels after swimming. The younger kids had gone home earlier.

Frieda smirked. "I guess I can tell now," she said. "Dad already sent his letter to the police."

"What letter? What police?" asked Trudy, in alarm.

"About those Japs. They've got a radio out there on Black Creek and they get orders straight from Japan!" Frieda said.

"You're crazy!" Trudy answered.

"My Dad heard them! Him and Jimmy Wallace. They snuck over there one night and heard Japanese talk from the radio."

"So what?" said Trudy. "It isn't a spy radio. I saw it. It's just like ours. Shigi told me there's a station in Vancouver that broadcasts in Japanese. It's not coming from Japan!"

Mary, who was lying on her back, wiggled her toes and stared at them for a moment. Then she squinted up at Trudy.

"It could be," she said. "You don't know what a spy radio looks like!"

Not Mary, too! Was everyone infected with hatred?

Trudy snorted. "I know the Nakanos aren't spies," she declared.

"You better watch out," Frieda said. "My Dad says if we're not careful, this whole province will be taken over by Orientals. They'll shove us all out."

Trudy just glared at her in disgust. Mary sat up, looking thoughtful.

"I wonder if that Japanese boy with my cousin upset the boat on purpose," she said.

Trudy jumped up and snapped her towel viciously.

"And drowned himself, too!" she said.

"Maybe," answered Frieda. "They're fanatics." Quickly, before the others could ask her what that word meant, she added, "That's what my Dad says."

But Trudy wasn't listening. She stomped home along the plank road. How could people be so dumb! When she first told Mary about the Nakano shrine where Skuli Johnson was remembered, Mary had been very touched. She even told Shigi she was sorry about his cousin. Now, all of a sudden, the Japanese who'd been living in camp for months were spies and killers? Again the memory of Tommy Moriyama talking in the secret room floated into her mind. She refused to think about it. Anyway, how come Mary was siding with Frieda? She was supposed to be Trudy's best friend. Was that going to change? Did she have to be mean to Shigi to keep Mary's friendship? Well, she wouldn't be! Suddenly she had a vision of herself always being alone, always on the outside of whatever was going on. Like Mum and her smelly fish lunches. It would be terrible. She ran up the porch steps, slammed both the front door and the bedroom door behind her and towelled her hair roughly. She didn't care what anybody thought! They were all wrong about the Japanese. She couldn't pretend to agree with them.

She tried to talk to her parents, but they told her to be patient.

"It will all blow over as soon as this trial is finished," Mum said. "We've been through it before. People are always ready to blame someone else for their troubles."

"But it's not fair!" said Trudy. "Dad, you know Mr. Nakano isn't a spy. Why don't you tell those dopes?"

"Trudy, I have to work with those guys. Why should I make enemies of them when the problem will solve itself anyway?"

"What do you mean?"

"Ken Nakano and the other men will be leaving soon."

She stared at him. "Leaving? Where are they going?"

"There's a logging company owned by a Japanese man up at Fanny Bay. He hires only Japanese. Ken Nakano told me they'd all been to see him last month. He'll hire them all."

"So that's where those men were on the cougar day!" said Trudy. "Nick Carley said they were at a big spy meeting up at the old mine."

Dad laughed. "That kid reads too many comic books. Who does he think they're spying for? Listen, Trudy, they've got a nice little community there at Fanny Bay. Quite a big school, I've heard. Lots of other Japanese women and kids. Your friends will be better off there."

How Trudy hated that phrase! Maybe Shigi would be happier up there, but he wouldn't forget the rotten way he'd been treated in Mellor's Camp.

Shigi didn't return to school. When Trudy asked about him, Miss Lewis said she had made out his report card so that he could register in his new school in the fall. Her parents told her that she couldn't go over to Black Creek.

"It's not that we believe the silly rumors, Trudy," said her mother. "I'm sure they don't want to talk to any of us. Besides you have to live here after they've gone. Think of the nasty names the kids would call you."

Who cared what Nick Carley said? Shigi was worth ten of him! How could she let the Japanese boy know that she was still his friend? After hours of thinking, she had a brilliant idea. She'd give him a present. What to give? He'd like more parts for his meccano set, but there was no time to go to the store in Milton and, anyway, she had no money. He wouldn't want any of her books. He liked baseball, but he already had a bat, ball and mitt. She had nothing a musician would want.

Oh, yes she did! The perfect gift!

Could she bear to part with it? It was her most treasured possession. Shigi knew that and he would understand that one person at least didn't hate him.

At supper, Dad poured milk on his bowl of bread pudding. He said, "The boss paid off the Japanese guys today. They're leaving tomorrow morning."

Trudy put down her spoon, braced her hands on the table and looked him straight in the eye.

"I'm giving Shigi my picture of Stan," she declared. "Can I take it over there tonight?"

Muriel gasped. Karl choked on a mouthful of pudding.

"You won't even let me touch it," he said when he could speak.

If she heard him, Trudy didn't answer. She was watching the long look exchanged between her parents.

Finally Dad spoke.

"No, you can't go over there." He held up his hand to stop Trudy's protest. "They are all going out together in Tommy's truck tomorrow morning. Probably at the crack of dawn. You and I will get up early and wait for them to pass."

Trudy, fearful of missing her chance, had a very restless night.

❧

On the same evening that Trudy was telling her parents she was going to give Shigi a gift, the Japanese family were preparing to move.

The big room was crowded with closed packing crates. The sleeping mats had been spread out for the last night in this house. Shigi's mother and Yumi were cleaning and wrapping the supper dishes to be placed in the last open box. His father was waiting to nail it shut.

Ken Nakano glanced up at his son. He was standing as if at attention holding a narrow box.

"Is that going in here?" Ken asked.

"No," answered Shigi. "I am going to give it to Trudy Paige."

His father's face darkened with anger. "You're not giving anything to one of them!"

Yumi, frightened at her father's tone, clutched her mother's skirt.

The woman looked from her son to her husband. Both had stubborn looks on their faces.

"What is it, son?" she asked. "Let me see."

Shigi placed the box on a crate. He lifted out a black display stand and a fan which he unfolded and set on the stand. The fan was made of thin strips of wood and painted with a scene of cherry blossoms and women in kimonos.

"You bought that for your mother's birthday next month!" said his father who had helped him choose it in Vancouver.

"I have nothing suitable for a girl," said Shigi. He bowed to his mother. "I will get you something else. This must be a gift for Trudy."

"After all they've done to us, you would give a gift?" yelled his father.

Shigi winced, but he spoke firmly. "Trudy has been my friend."

His mother put her arm around Yumi, still clinging to her skirt. "She saved our daughter from the cougar, husband," she said mildly.

The father's eyes darted to the little girl. His expression softened. He looked up at his wife and then at his son.

"Well. Well. We will ask Tommy to stop at their house. You may leave it on the porch."

Next morning, Tom Paige stumbled out of the bedroom at six o'clock. Trudy was setting the table.

"It's hardly light out there," he grumbled. "They're probably still in bed."

"You said the crack of dawn," answered Trudy. "I lit the fire and put the coffee on."

When he'd had a cup of coffee and two pieces of toast, Dad joined Trudy at the window overlooking the road. He put his hand on her shoulder.

"Ken Nakano is pretty bitter, girl," he warned. "He may not let Shigi take your parcel. They may not even stop."

"Oh, yes, they will," said Trudy. "Unless they want to run over me! Listen! A truck!"

"Put on your jacket! It's cold out there," called Dad, as Trudy wrestled with the door knob.

He waited behind a post on the porch while Trudy stood beside the road. She was shivering, partly from the cool air, partly from excitement and partly from fear that the Japanese would just keep going.

The truck was slowing. As the headlights swept over her, it stopped. She saw Mrs. Nakano and Yumi through the cab window.

Shigi jumped down from the back. He started with surprise when he saw her.

They stared at one another for a moment. Then they spoke together.

"I brought you a present."

They exchanged parcels. Tears of relief filled Trudy's eyes. When the driver called impatiently in Japanese, Shigi's father reached down and hauled him into the truck. It drove ahead.

"Goodbye," called Trudy.

"*Sayonara*," answered Shigi.

That means something like "Till we meet again" thought Trudy. It's not the same as "goodbye for ever." If Shigi's going to be an engineer and I become a teacher, we'll have to leave these little logging camps and go to high school. Maybe we will meet again and become real friends. She stood waving until the tail lights disappeared at the bridge.

Inside the house, Trudy opened her present. She set the fan on its stand and placed it on the top shelf of the sideboard where she had kept Stan's photo. She was happy that it was something very Japanese. Shigi did understand that she was his friend. And so would everyone else who saw the fan displayed in a place of honour among the family photos.

GLOSSARY

A-FRAME: An A-shaped frame of logs from which a block and tackle are suspended to hoist logs from or onto trucks or railroad flat cars.

BUNK HOUSE: a long building where the loggers slept and ate.

CAMP: the whole logging operation, as in Mellor's Camp

CHOKERMAN: logger who places wire rope around a log so that it can be pulled.

CRUMMY: car or bus to take logging crews to work areas in the woods.

DEPRESSION: a ten year period (1929-1939) when economic conditions were very difficult for most people in Canada.

DONKEY ENGINE: portable engine equipped with drums and cables used to move logs in the woods.

FIRST AID MAN: a logger specially trained to give medical help in emergencies.

FLATCAR: a railway car with no sides.

FLOATING CAMP: logging operation where the buildings were on rafts in the lake or bay of the sea.

FLUNKEY: person working in a cookhouse in a logging camp as waiter and/or dishwasher.

HIGH RIGGER: man who cuts off the limbs and top of a high tree and rigs it with pulleys so that logs can be lifted and pulled.

LOG DUMP: end of the road where logs are dropped at the sawmill.

LOGGED-OFF: all the trees have been cut.

LOGGER: man who works in the woods cutting or hauling logs.

MAINTENANCE GANG: men who keep the machinery in repair.

MISERY WHISTLE: nickname for the signal for an accident, often seven toots.

PLANING MILL: place where logs are cut into boards.

PLANK ROAD: a road made by laying two rows of planks on the ground.

QUITTING WHISTLE: signals the end of a shift.

RESCUE CREW: men specially trained to help loggers at accident sites.

RIDING THE RODS: during the Depression, many out-of-work men stole rides on the trains, climbing under the cars onto the "rods," or into open box cars.

RIGGING AND RE-RIGGING: fastening the hardware on a spar tree that then lifts other logs.

SAWMILL: where logs are made into lumber.

SHAY ENGINE: a type of railway engine widely used in early logging camps.

SHIGATAGANAI: Japanese word meaning, "There's nothing you can do about it." or "You can't change it, so accept it."

SPAR TREE: a tall tree that is used to support the hardware to hoist and move other logs.

SPARK CATCHER: a metal plate over the smokestack of a railway engine to deflect the sparks toward the ground.

SPARK WATCH: in very dry conditions, people watched the train to make sure a spark did not cause a fire.

SPEEDER: a railcar with a motor used on a railway track. Large varieties took loggers to the job site.

SPEEDERMAN: the man who ran the speeder.

WHISTLE PUNK: signalman. Communication in the woods was by whistle. The boss would tell the signalman how many toots of the whistle to signal for various movements such as the train coming or times such as the start of work.

WOODS OPERATION: logging in the forest.

ABOUT THE AUTHOR

Constance Horne was born in Winnipeg and lived in Manitoba until she moved to Nelson, B.C. where she met her husband. Later they moved to Vancouver and then to Victoria. After teaching high school for a few years, she became a stay-at-home mother.

As a student and teacher, Constance's favorite subject was Canadian history. She has visited historical sights in all ten provinces and one territory. Someday she hopes to travel to the rest of the North. For many years her dream was to write books for children that would teach them about the people of their own country. The chance to try finally came when the last child went to school. Her first book was published in 1989. Six more books followed.

Constance Horne and her husband live in Victoria, B.C. They have four grown-up children and two grandsons.